THE DAVENPORTS EAT

A GREEN HILLS COOKBOOK

VIRGINIA'DELE SMITH

Published by Books are Ubiquitous, Inc.
in the United States of America
booksareubiquitous.com

Books are Ubiquitous is a federally registered trademark.

Paperback ISBN: 978-1-957036-21-2

Titles by Virginia'dele Smith

Sadie & Sam: PART 1 - Introductory Short Story (FREE)
Book 0: My Manifesto - Short Memoir (FREE)

The Davenports
Book 1: Grocery Girl
Book 2: In the Trenches
Book 3: Three Times to Make Sure
Book 4: Take a Chance on Love

For my dad, Howard…Grandpa Howard

Whether together in the same room
or hundreds of miles apart,
I feel your love wherever we are.
I can't imagine this life
— nor this writing adventure —
without your optimism and encouragement,
your unwavering support,
and your brilliant contributions!

A WORD FROM ASHLI...

Happiness is a small house,
with a big kitchen.
Alfred Hitchcock

My family often teases that we could happily live in a one-room shack as long as we have a table to gather around and good food to eat. The four of us — my husband, myself, our son, and our daughter — share a special bond. I have no doubt we can tackle and conquer anything the world tosses our way!

It's true: we're that family that loves being together, and over the years we've spent countless hours divvying up jobs in the kitchen, cooking meals, trying new recipes, and sharing tidbits of life over breakfast, lunch, and dinner. Because we value our mealtimes so much, I'm quite passionate about cooking, baking, canning, collecting cookbooks, creating new recipes, and sharing our family favorites. I can't imagine *not* showering my loved ones with homemade treats, celebration feasts, and mouth-watering suppers. Pouring my heart into what I feed them brings me great joy.

They say to write what you know. So, when I began writing fiction a few years ago, including menus, describing cuisine, and highlighting the importance of food experiences in my wholesome and cozy romance novels made perfect sense to me.

I had no idea how much attention those book elements would garner, no notion that editors, book reviewers, and casual readers would be interested in them. I never dreamed I'd receive so many requests for the recipes I've compiled from friends, family, and experiments — the recipes I've been cooking and baking for years! But readers were interested, I dreamed, and now here it is: a collection of what the Davenports eat throughout the first four books of the Green Hills series.

From Maree's homemade strawberry jam and her comforting chicken spaghetti in *Grocery Girl*, to Maxwell and Janie Lyn's bread-making adventure from *In the Trenches*, to the Davenport's tradition of Mexican food for Christmas in *Three Times to Make Sure*, and to the mega trays of Brookies in *Take a Chance on Love*, great food has been a staple in my books. Now you can bring these Green Hills favorites into your home.

I hope you have a blast cooking with the characters. Please enjoy sharing their oohs and ahhs over the comfort foods and sweet delights found on the following pages. Have fun revisiting the excerpts from each book and going behind the scenes to learn why these recipes came to be in *The Davenports* miniseries.

I pray this collection inspires your family to spend time together — time planning, shopping, prepping, cooking, baking, plating, staging, eating, and yes, even cleaning the kitchen **together.**

*T*ime is a commodity we can't regenerate, so we must make the most of every moment with our true loves. What better way to accomplish that than with a marvelous meal?

*W*ith love and hugs,

Ashli
montgomery

CONTENTS

PLAN, PREP, AND MEASURE

Cooking is an art, and baking is a science.
Author unknown

Personally, I'm a "throw it together" kind of cook, but I know planning, prepping, and measuring are important when cooking *and* baking, so I included a few tips for each phase...

PLAN

When my kids were young and our schedules were particularly busy, I devised a fool-proof meal planning system that ensured we ate a variety of meals which included a diverse list of ingredients. When paired with the weekly grocery deals and coupons, the system also saves a lot of money. Best of all, the system alleviates stress of the dreaded *What's for Dinner?* question we all hate to hear.

- Print or draw a full year of blank calendar pages, one month per page.
- Label the columns of the calendar grid with a theme for each day of the week. My typical labels are *Sunday = Soup & Sandwiches, Monday = Slow Cooker, Tuesday = Chicken, Wednesday = Pasta, Thursday = Pork/Fish, Friday = Beef, and Saturday = Anything Goes*
- Fill in commitments that prevent dinner at home such as meetings, practices, work obligations, ball games, etc.
- Write dinner ideas under each column based on the theme for that day of the week. I find it easier to think of four slow cooker recipes, then four chicken dishes, then four pasta dishes, and so forth than it is to randomly think up thirty different meals on the fly. I'm always astonished at how quickly the squares fill up, and I often need multiple months' pages to exhaust all our favorites and any new recipes I want to try.

In no time, you'll have a full month of dinner ideas, and maybe more!

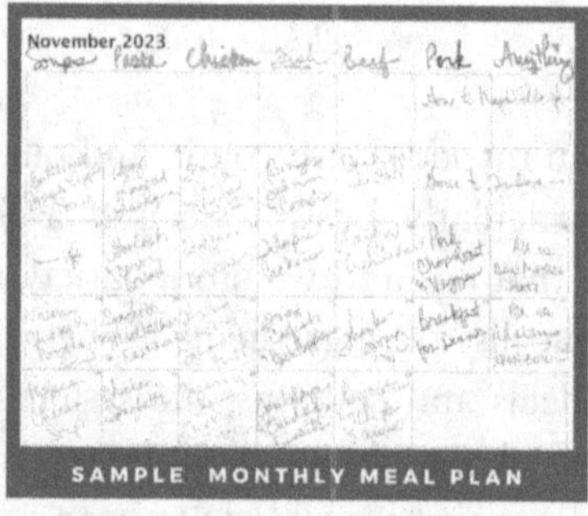

PREP

*M*ise en place is a French cooking term that means "everything in place" and defines how to prep for success when cooking and baking. Here are the key steps:

1. Check your recipe — make sure you have all the ingredients and pots, pans, and platters you'll need.

2. Collect your tools — things can get hectic in the kitchen; having all your tools on hand eliminates chaos and stress when everything's cooking and simmering and finishing at once.

3. Gather your ingredients — wash, measure, and cut your ingredients ahead of time so you aren't trying to do so in a pinch.

4. Organize your prepped items — now that everything is ready to cook, place prepped ingredients in small bowls and arrange them on your work space so everything you need is right at your fingertips.

MEASURE

To measure or not to measure, that is the question.

*W*ell, not exactly, but as I mentioned, I'm notorious for guesstimating as I toss in ingredients and spices. Luckily, it almost always turns out well, but I know without a doubt, measuring is better. Having a measurement guide close by is helpful and a great deterrent when I want to be lazy and skip this all-important step.

*H*ere's one that has everything I ever need…

MEASURING GUIDE

a dash = 8 drops (liquid) ≈ ⅛ teaspoon (slightly less)

1 teaspoon = 60 drops
3 teaspoons = 1 tablespoon = ½ fluid ounce

½ tablespoon = 1½ teaspoons
2 tablespoons (liquid) = 1 fluid ounce = ⅛ cup
3 tablespoons = 1½ fluid ounces = 1 jigger
4 tablespoons = ¼ cup

⅛ cup = 2 tablespoons
⅓ cup = 5 tablespoons + 1 teaspoon
1 cup = ½ pint = 8 fluid ounces
2 cups = 1 pint = 16 fluid ounces
4 cups = 1 quart = 2 pints = 32 fluid ounces
4 quarts = 1 gallon

1 peck = 8 quarts = 2 gallons
1 bushel = 4 pecks

*A*nd now… The Davenports EAT!

BREAKFAST

*Breakfast is a meal
with an incredible emotional charge.
It's a feeling of fellowship that is unlike
any other meal of the day.*
Anthony Bourdain

Skipping breakfast is all the trend these days, but it's not for me. I need a bite of something to get my thoughts flowing and my motivation rolling for the day. But that's personal preference, and if you don't do an early meal, these recipes work well as *Breakfast for Dinner,* which is always a treat.

However and whenever you decide to serve them, your family and friends are sure to delight in these breakfast dishes!

AVOCADO TOAST

Book 4: Take a Chance on Love
Chapter 9

"How did you know that?" Landry asked when the woman had walked away.

"How did I know what?" Davis countered.

"What I like to order." She sat dumbfounded.

"It's what you always order when you're tired."

"When I'm tired? What do I order for breakfast when I'm not tired?" Landry asked, crossing her arms and leaning back to see what he'd come up with.

"Let's see... French toast sprinkled with powdered sugar — no syrup — when you're excited to have a day off and there's nothing scheduled that you have to do. An omelet with two eggs, ham, mushrooms, diced onions, and bell pepper — no cheese — when you have a lot of studying planned *for the day. And when breakfast turns into brunch, avocado toast with a fried egg on top — over easy — with a side salad and cranberry juice instead of hot tea." On that note, he crossed his arms, leaning back to mimic her posture.*

She didn't know how to respond.

———

This part in the book is inspired by the movie *Win a Date with Tad Hamilton*, when Pete explains Rosalee's six smiles. It's such a sweet scene! And it's a powerful way to show exactly how much one character cherishes another. There's no way Davis knows that much about Landry without being hopelessly in love with her… Too bad he doesn't realize it quite yet.

<u>INGREDIENTS</u>

2 Haas avocados, ripe but not mushy
8 cherry tomatoes, diced
¼ teaspoon Kosher salt
⅛ teaspoon ground black pepper
⅛ teaspoon garlic powder
4 slices bread, toasted and lightly buttered
4 eggs, scrambled, fried, or poached
4 tablespoons strawberry jam
⅛ teaspoon dill

<u>INSTRUCTIONS</u>

1. SLICE AVOCADOS IN HALF, REMOVE PIT, AND SPOON THE AVOCADOS INTO A MIXING BOWL.
2. MASH AVOCADOS UNTIL CREAMY AND SMOOTH USING A SPOON, FORK, OR POTATO MASHER.
3. ADD TOMATOES, SALT, PEPPER, AND GARLIC POWDER TO MIXING BOWL AND STIR WELL.
4. SCOOP ¼ OF THE AVOCADO MIXTURE ON A SLICE OF TOAST. REPEAT FOR ALL FOUR SLICES OF TOAST.
5. TOP EACH SLICE OF AVOCADO-SMEARED BREAD WITH ONE EGG, PREPPED AS DESIRED.
6. DOLLOP ¼ OF THE JAM ON EACH SLICE AND GARNISH WITH A PINCH OF DILL.

BLUEBERRY SCONES

Book 1: Grocery Girl
Chapter 4

*he three of them — Janie Lyn, Maree, and Miss Sadie —
had just filled their plates to enjoy a late afternoon snack of
blueberry scones with clotted cream and fresh berries left over from Maree's
fruit delivery a couple days earlier that week.*

*Like the phenomenal hostess she is, Miss Sadie always has a snack
baked and ready at Marshall Mansion. She serves these scrumptious
scones with clotted cream and fresh berries when a rare afternoon finds
Maree, Landry, and Janie Lyn all at the house together.*

———

his scone recipe is simple to make and works well
with any add-in such as another fruit or even something savory. For best results, invest in a pastry cutter for the
butter and leave yourself at least an hour for the dough to chill
in the refrigerator before baking.

Note: Another version of this recipe is found later in *The Davenports* miniseries…

Book 3: Three Times to Make Sure
Chapter 36

She fixed a cup of tea, heaped clotted cream and fresh jam on two raisin scones, slid her arms into her heavy coat, grabbed her journal, and headed for the table where the sun shone bright warmth on the back patio.

———

To try M'Kenzee and Bren's version of this delightful breakfast, substitute one cup of raisins for the blueberries in this recipe.

<u>INGREDIENTS</u>

2 CUPS FLOUR

½ CUP SUGAR

2½ TEASPOONS BAKING POWDER

½ TEASPOON BAKING SODA

½ TEASPOON SALT

1 TEASPOON CINNAMON

½ CUP BUTTER (CUBED AND KEPT VERY COLD)

1¼ CUP FRESH BLUEBERRIES

¾ CUP HEAVY CREAM (KEPT VERY COLD)

1 TEASPOON VANILLA EXTRACT

<u>INSTRUCTIONS</u>

1. WHISK FLOUR, SUGAR, BAKING POWDER, BAKING SODA, SALT, AND CINNAMON TOGETHER IN A LARGE MIXING BOWL.

2. CUT BUTTER CUBES INTO DRY MIX USING A PASTRY CUTTER OR FORK. AVOID USING YOUR HANDS BECAUSE THE BUTTER NEEDS TO STAY VERY COLD UNTIL IT GOES INTO THE OVEN. BUTTER SHOULD BE CRUMBLY BUT STILL VISIBLE WHEN FINISHED CUTTING IT IN.

3. ADD BLUEBERRIES TO MIXTURE. STIR GENTLY, JUST UNTIL THEY'RE SCATTERED THROUGHOUT THE MIXTURE.

4. USE A SPOON TO CREATE A WELL OR CRATER IN THE MIDDLE OF THE MIXTURE. POUR THE CREAM AND VANILLA EXTRACT INTO THE WELL. STIR GENTLY UNTIL MIXTURE IS DOUGH-LIKE AND MOIST.

5. TURN DOUGH ONTO A FLAT SURFACE AND LIGHTLY KNEAD INTO A BALL.

6. USING A ROLLING PIN, FLATTEN DOUGH BALL FROM CENTER TO CREATE A 1-INCH THICK CIRCLE.

7. SLICE THE CIRCLE INTO EIGHTHS (LIKE A PIZZA) AND PLACE EACH TRIANGLE ON A LINED COOKIE SHEET (I LIKE TO LINE WITH PARCHMENT PAPER OR A SILICONE BAKING MAT).

8. COVER AND PLACE COOKIE SHEET INTO THE REFRIGERATOR TO CHILL FOR AT LEAST ONE HOUR.

9. BAKE AT 400°F FOR TWENTY MINUTES OR UNTIL LIGHTLY GOLDEN.

10. SERVE WITH JAM AND CLOTTED CREAM.

BRUNCH ON A BUN

Book 2: In the Trenches
Chapter 4

Janie Lyn had been riding a bus as far as she could get from home, planning to go all the way to the West Coast. But when the bus stopped in Tulsa, Oklahoma, along Route 66, she'd felt called to take a break from running.

She'd walked downtown from the bus station, discovering a thread of hope and a sense of foundation she hadn't expected to find anywhere. Even though it was just past noon, Janie Lyn craved breakfast and had just ordered a sandwich best described as brunch — a fried egg with lettuce, tomato, avocado, and bacon on a croissant — and a cinnamon roll for dessert when two ladies in the booth behind her started talking about a quilting retreat they were excited to attend that weekend. They talked about a lakeside resort in a town called Green Hills. The two women painted an image in Janie Lyn's mind of a magical place where the people were caring and kind and where the pace of life allowed one to breathe. Their descriptions of the thick green trees and the sparkling water on the lake sounded like a dream. Their plan to sit on the dock in old wooden rocking chairs, watching the sun set each night as they sipped a glass of wine and listened to the cicadas was the final straw. Janie Lyn had to see this mystical town and its purported beauty.

———

The breakfast sandwich Janie Lyn enjoys in Tulsa is a real thing. Years ago I ordered it at the Dilly Diner, and it was so amazing I had to figure out how to make my own version at home. I've switched out a few items to make it just the way I like it, but as with all wonderful sandwiches, perfection is in the eye of the builder, so make it your own creation of messy goodness!

INGREDIENTS

1 OVERSIZED CROISSANT

½ TEASPOON DIJON MUSTARD

½ TEASPOON CREAM CHEESE, SOFTENED

DASH OF CELERY SALT

SALT & PEPPER

3 STRIPS OF BACON, BAKED OR FRIED TO TASTE

2–3 SLICES OF TOMATO

½ AN AVOCADO, SLICED

1 TEASPOON CAPERS

1 EGG, FRIED TO TASTE

<u>INSTRUCTIONS</u>

1. SLICE CROISSANT IN HALF LIKE A HAMBURGER BUN.
2. SPREAD MUSTARD ON ONE HALF AND SOFTENED CREAM CHEESE ON THE OTHER.
3. STACK REMAINING INGREDIENTS ON BOTTOM HALF OF BUN IN ORDER OF LIST.
4. REPLACE TOP OF BUN AND DIG IN. EXTRA NAPKINS COME HIGHLY RECOMMENDED (FROM EXPERIENCE).

CINNAMON ROLLS

"Do I smell cinnamon rolls?"

"That you do," Janie Lyn answered with a big grin. "Not the breakfast of champions, but it's become Max's favorite… I'm certain the team nutritionist wouldn't be too happy." She placed a huge pastry on a plate and set the plate on the bar for M'Kenzee. "But he's really hard to say no to," Janie Lyn added with a stage whisper. "Just don't tell him I said so. Pretty please?"

"Your secret is safe with me," M'Kenzee promised. "Although you might not be fooling anyone. It's pretty obvious you like him."

———

Cinnamon rolls (sometimes called *cinnamon buns* in the Green Hills novels) make frequent appearances because I love them very much.

I chose this particular scene to represent them in my first Green Hills cookbook because its inspiration is extra special to me…

As a college football coach, my husband mentors and affects the lives of young men in significant ways. In my own tiny way, I get to help because Coach and I provide an example of what a strong, sound, respectful marriage looks like between two people who — almost thirty years in — are still hopelessly devoted and ridiculously in love with one another. It's truly a gift!

An example of that took place one Thanksgiving when the football team and coaches' families were enjoying a feast together. Coach playfully teased me saying he had it "so rough" at home with a wife that likes to —and I quote— "crack the whip" if he steps out of line. The players listening laughed, every one of them knowing I'm totally head over heels for Coach Monty. Then one of the guys countered with a soft chuckle and said in an understated tone, "I don't know, Coach… I think she likes you."

That young man overcame some tough obstacles in life. He's now blissfully married to a smart and stunning woman, and together they have a beautiful family. They are building a strong, sound, respectful marriage of their own. Knowing that young man is in such a good place is an answered prayer.

I've never forgotten how my heart hummed at the compliment I felt that day, and I'd venture to guess his wife "likes" him, too!

DOUGH INGREDIENTS

4 CUPS ALL-PURPOSE FLOUR
⅓ GRANULATED SUGAR
½ SALT
1 CUP WHOLE MILK
4 TABLESPOONS SALTED BUTTER
3 TEASPOONS YEAST
1 LARGE EGG
NONSTICK COOKING SPRAY

FILLING INGREDIENTS

¼ CUP SALTED BUTTER
½ CUP BROWN SUGAR
1 TABLESPOON CINNAMON

ICING INGREDIENTS

3 CUPS POWDERED SUGAR
⅓ CUP HEAVY CREAM
1 ½ TEASPOONS VANILLA EXTRACT

INSTRUCTIONS

1. MEASURE AND SET OUT MILK, BUTTER, AND EGG TO ALLOW TIME FOR EACH TO REACH ROOM TEMPERATURE.
2. MAKE THE DOUGH USING A LARGE MIXING BOWL. STIR FLOUR, SUGAR, AND SALT TOGETHER.

3. Using the microwave, heat milk and butter in a small glass bowl or measuring cup. Go in small intervals and heat ONLY until warm to touch.

4. Stir yeast into milk and melted butter until completely dissolved.

5. Pour liquid mixture into dry ingredients.

6. Add egg and stir until well blended and dough forms.

7. Knead the dough on a lightly floured work surface for 4–5 minutes to create a small ball.

8. Spray a sheet of plastic wrap with nonstick cooking spray. cover dough ball with the plastic wrap, sprayed side against the dough. Let sit for about 10 minutes.

9. After the time is up, begin to work the dough ball into a 15" x 10" rectangle on the lightly floured workspace.

10. Spread filling butter across the dough rectangle.

11. Top with brown sugar.

12. Follow with a coating of cinnamon.

13. Roll the dough to create a 15" log.

14. Using dental floss, sewing thread, or a very sharp knife, slice the log into 12 even pinwheels, being careful not to squish the dough flat.

15. Place pinwheels flat in a large pie pan or baking dish.

16. Cover the pinwheels with a tea towel for one hour or until dough rises double in size.

17. Remove tea towel and bake at 375°F for 20–

25 MINUTES OR UNTIL DOUGH IS GOLDEN BROWN ON TOP AND NO LONGER GOOEY INSIDE THE ROLLS.

18. WHEN READY, REMOVE ROLLS FROM OVEN. LET SIT FOR 5 MINUTES WHILE STIRRING ALL THREE ICING INGREDIENTS TOGETHER WITH A FORK UNTIL ICING IS SMOOTH AND CREAMY.

19. FROST ABOUT ⅓ OF THE ICING MIXTURE ONTO THE HOT ROLLS.

20. LET ROLLS COOL FOR ANOTHER 7–8 MINUTES. THEN DRIZZLE REMAINING ICING IN A ZIG-ZAG PATTERN ACROSS THE ROLLS.

21. SERVE CINNAMON ROLLS WHILE STILL WARM.

FRITTATA OLÉ

Book 1: Grocery Girl
Chapter 2

"With that many eggs on your list and all these veggies, it looks like you might be making a frittata," she said. "Grab a plastic bag right there; these are all wet from the spray." Then she shook out a bunch of long, flat dark-green leaves.

"Who knows," he said, "I—"

"Larsen, let's go," one of the guys hollered from the cashier's stand.

"—guess I better go," he continued, smoothly switching gears midsentence. "Thanks for the help…" He paused for her to fill in her name as she dropped the greens into the bag.

"Maree," she provided, looking up into those mystical gray eyes. "Maree Davenport."

———

*T*his is the scene that kept me awake at night — on and off for about two years — before I found the courage to put my book idea onto paper. Placing a traditional romance-genre "meet cute" in the produce aisle of the Get'n'Go still brings a smile to my face, and I love how Maree and Rhys's courageous love story set the tone for all my Green Hills novels to come!

*E*ven with the dinosaur kale thrown in, this hearty breakfast bake is one my family requests on a regular basis, so I know your crew will devour it, too.

INGREDIENTS

3 CUPS CORN TORTILLA CHIPS, CRUSHED

16-OUNCE JAR SALSA VERDE

2 TABLESPOONS OLIVE OIL

1 MEDIUM ONION

1 LARGE POBLANO PEPPER

1 GARLIC CLOVE, PRESSED

2 TABLESPOONS FRESH CILANTRO, SNIPPED (OPTIONAL)

1 CUP COOKED CHICKEN, DICED OR SHREDDED

1 BUNCH LACINATO (ALSO CALLED DINOSAUR KALE), WASHED

12 EGGS

¾ CUP MILK

10 OUNCES QUESO FRESCO

1 ROMA TOMATO, SLICED

4 OUNCES SOUR CREAM

CLASSIC CATALINA DRESSING

4 OUNCES MEXICAN BLEND SHREDDED CHEESE

<u>INSTRUCTIONS</u>

1. COMBINE CRUSHED CHIPS AND FULL JAR OF SALSA VERDE IN A LARGE MIXING BOWL. SET ASIDE ALLOWING TIME FOR CHIPS TO ABSORB THE SALSA.
2. IN A SKILLET, SAUTE ONION IN OLIVE OIL FOR TWO MINUTES.
3. ADD KALE. COOK FOR 40 MINUTES OR UNTIL KALE IS FULLY WILTED AND BEGINNING TO GET CRUNCHY.
4. ADD PEPPER, GARLIC, AND CHICKEN TO THE SKILLET. CONTINUE TO COOK FOR THREE MINUTES.
5. REMOVE SKILLET FROM HEAT.
6. IN ANOTHER MIXING BOWL, WHISK EGGS, MILK, AND CILANTRO TOGETHER. ADD MILK MIXTURE TO SOAKED TORTILLA CHIPS AND STIR WELL.
7. POUR EGG AND CHIP MIXTURE INTO SKILLET. DO NOT STIR INGREDIENTS.
8. CRUMBLE QUESO FRESCO EVENLY OVER TOP OF FRITTATA.
9. BAKE AT 350°F FOR 25–30 MINUTES OR UNTIL EGG MIXTURE IS SET IN CENTER. REMOVE FROM OVEN.
10. PLACE TOMATO SLICES ON TOP AND LET STAND FOR FIVE MINUTES.
11. SERVE FRITTATA WITH A DOLLOP OF SOUR CREAM, A RIBBON OF CATALINA, AND A SPRINKLING OF SHREDDED CHEESE.

HOMEMADE GRANOLA

Book 2: In the Trenches
Chapter 10

She was pulling a baking sheet of homemade granola out of the oven when he entered the kitchen.

"Good morning," he said, walking to the coffeepot with a jaunty bounce in his step.

"Hi," she said without looking his way. That felt safer. Looking at him could be dangerous. Making eye contact might be lethal.

"This looks great!" Maxwell stood in awe of the fresh fruit, yogurt, light and fluffy scrambled eggs, and sizzling bacon set out buffet-style on the breakfast table. "I'm a big fan of breakfast, but my eggs and bacon never look quite like this."

Janie Lyn transferred the granola into a bowl, then picked up a pot of syrup simmering on the cooktop and drizzled it over the oats, grains, raisins, and dried cranberries. She stirred the glaze into the granola, sprinkled sugar and cinnamon on top, and set it on the table with the yogurt.

"I hope you enjoy it." She added a cereal bowl to the single place setting at the table.

"This is all for me?" he asked.

"Of course."

———

I had a ton of fun hinting at Janie Lyn's prowess in the kitchen throughout Book 1, so I had to include several examples of her incredible talent as a chef in Book 2.

It wasn't hard to accomplish when Maxwell is such a willing and eager taste-tester for anything — and *everything* — she makes!

<u>INGREDIENTS</u>

4 CUPS ROLLED OATS

1 CUP SLICED ALMONDS

1 CUP CHOPPED PECANS

1 CUP CHOPPED WALNUTS

½ CUP CHOPPED HAZELNUTS

½ CUP PUMPKIN SEEDS

⅛ TEASPOON KOSHER SALT

1 CUP RAISINS

1 CUP DRIED CRANBERRIES

1 CUP HONEY

1 CUP BROWN SUGAR

¼ CUP OLIVE OIL

¼ CUP COCONUT OIL

2 TABLESPOONS MAPLE SYRUP

2 TABLESPOONS VANILLA EXTRACT

2 TEASPOONS GROUND CINNAMON

1 TEASPOON GROUND NUTMEG

CINNAMON AND GRANULATED SUGAR FOR GARNISH

INSTRUCTIONS

1. COMBINE OATS, ALMONDS, PECANS, WALNUTS, HAZELNUTS, PUMPKIN SEEDS, AND SALT IN A LARGE MIXING BOWL. SPREAD MIXTURE EVENLY ACROSS A LARGE JELLY ROLL PAN.

2. ROAST NUT MIXTURE IN OVEN AT 350°F FOR SEVEN MINUTES.

3. REMOVE THE PAN FROM THE OVEN AND IMMEDIATELY TRANSFER NUT MIXTURE INTO A BOWL TO AVOID OVERCOOKING ON THE HOT PAN.

4. ADD THE RAISINS AND DRIED CRANBERRIES TO THE MIXTURE.

5. IN A SMALL SAUCEPAN, WHISK TOGETHER HONEY, BROWN SUGAR, OLIVE OIL, COCONUT OIL, MAPLE SYRUP, VANILLA EXTRACT, CINNAMON, AND NUTMEG AND BRING TO A SLOW SIMMER OVER MEDIUM HEAT.

6. WHEN MIXTURE BEGINS TO THICKEN SLIGHTLY, DRIZZLE OVER NUT MIXTURE.

7. SPRINKLE A LITTLE EXTRA CINNAMON AND SUGAR ON TOP.

8. LET COOL FOR A FEW MINUTES BEFORE SERVING. LET GRANOLA COOL AND DRY COMPLETELY BEFORE PACKAGING FOR STORAGE.

JACQUELINE'S BREAKFAST PIZZA

Book 4: Take a Chance on Love
Chapter 22

"Something smells good," Davis called out from his room, seconds before Landry and Zane watched him emerge down the hall.

Earlier that morning, he'd lumbered home from work, inhaled half a pan of his mom's breakfast pizza, and gone straight to bed. Four hours later, his voice, warm with lingering sleepiness, caused a flush of heat Landry tried to disregard. The sight of him tugging a soft t-shirt over his head to cover a washboard set of hard abs caused a flutter in her pulse she couldn't ignore.

———

Davis is all about food, and he loves, loves, loves home cooking!

His mom makes this quick and easy breakfast casserole for Landry and Zane one Tuesday morning, and Davis is happy to finish off the pan when he gets home from a long and exhausting shift at Fire Station #2.

If your family manages to leave any leftovers, you'll be happy to know they freeze very well for up to a month.

INGREDIENTS

3 ENGLISH MUFFINS, SLICED IN HALF

1 POUND BREAKFAST SAUSAGE, BROWNED

6 EGGS

$\frac{1}{4}$ MILK

1 CUP SHARP CHEDDAR CHEESE, GRATED

SALT & PEPPER

NONSTICK COOKING SPRAY

INSTRUCTIONS

1. COAT THE BOTTOM AND SIDES OF A 9" x 13" BAKING DISH WITH NONSTICK COOKING SPRAY.
2. LINE THE BOTTOM OF THE DISH WITH THE SIX ENGLISH MUFFIN HALVES, INSIDE OF THE MUFFIN FACING UP.
3. TOP BREAD WITH BROWNED SAUSAGE.
4. IN A SMALL BOWL, WHISK EGGS AND MILK TOGETHER. SEASON MIXTURE WITH SALT AND PEPPER TO TASTE.
5. POUR EGG MIXTURE OVER SAUSAGE.
6. TOP WITH GRATED CHEESE.
7. BAKE AT 375°F FOR 15–20 MINUTES OR UNTIL EGGS ARE COOKED THROUGH AND NO LONGER RUNNY.
8. SERVE WITH KETCHUP, SALSA, OR CREAM GRAVY.

TRIPLE T'S BREAKFAST BURRITOS

Book 3: Three Times to Make Sure
Chapter 27

"Good morning, intruders," she said, alerting the couple kissing in her kitchen that they were no longer alone.

Maree tried to jump out of Rhys's arms, but he held tight, placing one last peck on her forehead before picking up the drill to detach another cabinet door from its hinges.

"I brought breakfast. And muscle," Maree beamed.

"So I see," M'Kenzee teased while sifting through the white paper sack next to the sink. "Breakfast burritos? These smell so good," she admitted.

"Triple T's," Rhys told her. "The best in town."

———

hese are soooo good! Some might even say addictive, and they're my husband's specialty. It's a treat when he's home to make them because I have the double honor of not cooking while thoroughly enjoying the fruits of someone else's labor!

n the book, Earl sends "salt, pepper, salsa, ketchup, and hot sauce" to top them off, although, I'll admit, they're delicious all by themselves.

<u>INGREDIENTS</u>

1 DOZEN FLOUR TORTILLAS
1 POUND BACON
6 EGGS
¼ MILK
6 SMALL POTATOES, PEELED AND DICED
1 CUP GRATED CHEESE
SALT & PEPPER

<u>INSTRUCTIONS</u>

1. FRY BACON IN SKILLET UNTIL DONE TO YOUR PREFERENCE.
2. SET STRIPS ON A PAPER TOWELED PLATE TO ABSORB THE GREASE.
3. USE RESERVE BACON GREASE IN SKILLET TO FRY THE POTATOES UNTIL SOFT AND LIGHTLY BROWNED ON THE EDGES.
4. SET POTATOES ASIDE IN A BOWL.
5. IN A SMALL BOWL, WHISK EGGS AND MILK TOGETHER. SEASON MIXTURE WITH SALT AND PEPPER.
6. SCRAMBLE EGGS IN SKILLET.
7. ADD GRATED CHEESE AND POTATOES BACK TO SKILLET WHEN EGGS ARE FINISHED. WARM MIXTURE OVER LOW HEAT FOR 5–7 MINUTES.
8. WRAP TORTILLAS IN DAMP PAPER TOWEL AND WARM IN MICROWAVE FOR 90 SECONDS.
9. FILL WARM TORTILLAS WITH MIXTURE, ADD A STRIP OR TWO OF BACON, AND FOLD BURRITO.
10. TOP AS DESIRED.

SOUPS & STEWS

Soup is a lot like a family.
Each ingredient enhances the others;
each batch has its own characteristics;
and it needs time to simmer to reach full flavor.
Marge Kennedy

Don't be surprised if someday we have an entire Green Hills cookbook dedicated to soups and stews. For now, however, I've limited myself to sharing one recipe from each of the four Davenport miniseries books. Enjoy!

BUTTERNUT SQUASH & APPLE SOUP

Book 1: Grocery Girl
Chapter 12

The next course was a butternut squash and apple soup with cinnamon agrodolce. "Rich, but not too sweet, even with the cooked apples," an older woman at their table said with approval...

————

I could eat soup every day of the year, but I especially love wrapping my hands around a warm ceramic bowl in the autumn and winter when it's chilly and crisp outside. Maree attends the Fireman's Ball as Rhys's date on a night just like that, and this soup is but one of the scrumptious courses in which she delights during her magical Cinderella night.

etermined to create a sweet yet filling butternut squash soup, this recipe came about from my own trial and error. Depending on the size of the apples and onions, I tend to add more or less as needed to use up what I have in the kitchen. I also season to taste because I've found that no two batches of soup come out exactly the same!

PS: Agrodolce — Italian for sour (agro) and sweet (dolce) — is a sticky sauce traditionally made with pine nuts and a variety of dried fruits such as raisins, apricots, or currants. The sour comes from an acidic base such as vinegar or cider, and the sweet comes from reduced honey or sugar.

<u>INGREDIENTS</u>

½ STICK BUTTER

1 LARGE YELLOW ONION, CHOPPED

1 CLOVE GARLIC, MINCED

2 MEDIUM BUTTERNUT SQUASH, SEEDED AND CUBED

1 LARGE GRANNY SMITH APPLE, PEELED AND SLICED

1 LARGE RED DELICIOUS APPLE, PEELED AND SLICED

1 CUP GOLDEN RAISINS

1 CUP APPLE CIDER

4 CUPS CHICKEN BROTH

⅓ CUP BROWN SUGAR

½ CUP HONEY

¾ TEASPOON SALT

½ TEASPOON PEPPER

1 CUP HEAVY CREAM

1 TEASPOON GROUND CINNAMON
½ GROUND GINGER
¼ GROUND NUTMEG
¼ GROUND CLOVES
8-OUNCE TUB OF SOUR CREAM
3 TABLESPOONS FRESH CHIVES, CHOPPED FOR GARNISH

INSTRUCTIONS

1. MELT BUTTER IN A DUTCH OVEN OR LARGE STOCK POT. SAUTE ONION IN BUTTER FOR TWO MINUTES. ADD GARLIC FOR TWO MINUTES.
2. ADD SQUASH, APPLES, RAISINS, CIDER, BROTH, BROWN SUGAR, HONEY, SALT, AND PEPPER. COVER AND HEAT TO BOILING.
3. REDUCE HEAT AND SIMMER FOR THIRTY MINUTES.
4. CAREFULLY, USE AN IMMERSION BLENDER TO PROCESS SOUP UNTIL SMOOTH.
5. ADD CREAM, CINNAMON, GINGER, NUTMEG, AND CLOVES. RETURN TO BOIL FOR THREE TO FIVE MINUTES.
6. SERVE WITH A DOLLOP OF SOUR CREAM AND A SPRINKLING OF CHOPPED CHIVES.

CHILLED GAZPACHO

Book 2: In the Trenches
Chapter 3

"If I'd been paying any attention when I poured my tea the first time, I'd have known without a doubt that someone much more cultured than I was living here!"

$\mathcal{J}$anie Lyn is mortified when Max arrives home unannounced to find her living in his house.
But Max is thrilled!

$\mathcal{A}$lthough this recipe isn't mentioned specifically in the book, I envision it in a quart-sized jar next to the fresh fruits and vegetables Max mentions noticing in his fridge. Served cold on a warm day, this recipe is refreshing and energizing. And it's incredibly healthy, which can't be bad for a professional football player who loves cinnamon rolls and apple pies!

I found a version of this recipe online many years ago. Over time, I've tweaked it to become one I enjoy making several times each year. Not a fan of spicy foods, I leave out the jalepeño peppers; toss them back in to add some heat.

W hen hosting an event, I serve these in eight-ounce jelly jars to show off colorful summer veggies. Ahead of time, I tie a ribbon around the metal ring to attach a spoon. Then I set a basket or tray of soup jars in the fridge to chill until time to eat.

<u>**INGREDIENTS**</u>

3 LARGE SLICING TOMATOES, PEELED AND DICED

3 ROMA TOMATOES, PEELED AND DICED

1 YELLOW TOMATO, PEELED AND DICED

1 ORANGE TOMATO, PEELED AND DICED

2 CUCUMBERS, PEELED AND DICED

1 BUNCH GREEN ONIONS, CHOPPED

3 BELL PEPPERS (VARIETY OF COLORS), DICED

1 TABLESPOON MINCED GARLIC

1-2 JALAPEÑOS, SEEDED AND MINCED (OPTIONAL)

$\frac{1}{4}$ TEASPOON DRIED OREGANO

$\frac{1}{4}$ TEASPOON CAYENNE PEPPER

$\frac{1}{2}$ TEASPOON GROUND BLACK PEPPER

$\frac{1}{2}$ TEASPOON GROUND CUMIN

1 TEASPOON SALT
1 PINT CHERRY TOMATOES, CUT IN HALF
¼ CUP OLIVE OIL
1 TABLESPOON BALSAMIC VINEGAR
1 TABLESPOON WORCESTERSHIRE SAUCE
1 LIME, JUICED

INSTRUCTIONS

1. MIX DICED TOMATOES, CUCUMBERS, ONION, AND ALL PEPPERS IN A MIXING BOWL. ADD OREGANO, CAYENNE, BLACK PEPPER, CUMIN, AND SALT TO THE BOWL. MIX WELL.
2. IN A BLENDER, PURÉE CHERRY TOMATOES, OLIVE OIL, VINEGAR, WORCESTERSHIRE SAUCE, AND LIME JUICE UNTIL LIQUID IS STRAINABLE.
3. ADD LIQUID MIXTURE TO VEGETABLE MIX BY POURING IT THROUGH A STRAINER. STIR INGREDIENTS TOGETHER IN BOWL.
4. FILLING THE BLENDER ⅔ FULL, PURÉE SOUP MIXTURE IN BATCHES TO PROCESS SOUP.
5. USING A CANNING FUNNEL, LADLE SOUP INTO JARS, COVER, AND CHILL FOR AT LEAST THREE HOURS BEFORE SERVING SOUP COLD.

CREAMY CHICKEN NOODLE SOUP

Book 4: Take a Chance on Love
Chapter 2

After her late breakfast, Landry made up her bed, took a quick shower, and threw her wintertime lake essentials in a tote bag: a wool quilt, her favorite beanie and gloves, and two books — the one she'd already begun and a backup just in case she finished the first one too quickly. She called the hospital at Green Country Medical Center where she was in her final year of residency to tell Ruthie, the charge nurse and supervisor on duty, that she'd be away from her phone for the day but out at the lake so they could reach her via Audrie Boucher at Lakeside Yoga. Miss Sadie handed her a gigantic picnic basket filled with sandwiches, two tall thermoses of hot soup, bagged chips, fresh fruit, and still-warm peanut butter cookies.

———

*W*hen I'm too lazy to run to the store, I have a habit of throwing everything but the kitchen sink into a meal. I imagine Miss Sadie did the same thing when putting together Landry's picnic basket for a day at Daisy Lake.

This version of chicken noodle soup came about in such a way, when a big pot of soup sounded divine but it was too cold and blustery to venture out to buy groceries. It was so tasty I immediately wrote down (to the best of my memory) what I'd tossed in the pot so I could make it again…and again.

Since then, it's become a go-to, quick and easy recipe I love to serve with Toasties — leftover dinner rolls sliced, buttered, and toasted under the broiler. If I'm feeling industrious, I'll add a green salad on the side and perhaps an apple turnover — or peanut butter cookies — for dessert.

<u>INGREDIENTS</u>

1 STICK BUTTER
1 LARGE WHITE ONION, CHOPPED
1 ROTISSERIE CHICKEN, SHREDDED
(OR ABOUT 2 CUPS LEFTOVER CHICKEN, DICED)
1 TABLESPOON MRS. DASH®
1 BUNCH CELERY, CHOPPED
1 POUND CARROTS, PEELED AND CHOPPED
1 CAN WHOLE KERNEL CORN
(OR 16-OUNCE BAG FROZEN CORN)
4-OUNCE JAR PIMENTOS
1 CAN CREAM OF MUSHROOM SOUP
1 CAN CREAM OF CHICKEN SOUP
1 CAN CREAM OF POTATO SOUP
32-OUNCE CARTON CHICKEN BROTH
12-OUNCE CAN EVAPORATED MILK
12-OUNCE BAG WIDE EGG NOODLES
SALT & PEPPER

<u>INSTRUCTIONS</u>

1. MELT BUTTER IN A DUTCH OVEN OR LARGE STOCK POT. SAUTE ONION IN BUTTER FOR TWO MINUTES.
2. ADD CHICKEN AND MRS. DASH® TO ONIONS AND COOK FOR THREE MINUTES, STIRRING TO COAT CHICKEN IN BUTTER AND SEASONING.
3. ADD REMAINING INGREDIENTS.
4. COVER AND HEAT TO BOILING.
5. BOIL FOR SEVEN MINUTES OR UNTIL NOODLES ARE DONE TO DESIRED TEXTURE.
6. REDUCE HEAT AND SIMMER FOR ABOUT TWENTY MINUTES OR UNTIL CARROTS ARE SOFT BUT NOT YET FALLING APART.
7. SERVE HOT.

MEXICAN CHEESE SOUP

Book 3: Three Times to Make Sure
Chapter 16

Max trudged out in the weather to retrieve M'Kenzee and whatever had kept her so engrossed all day. He gathered the box, closing the lid and tucking everything under his arm. He pulled M'Kenzee to her feet, huddled her under his free arm, and nudged her toward the house.

"I didn't know. It's snowing," she marveled.

"Yes, it is," he muttered. "And the temperature dropped about twenty degrees in the last half hour. Janie Lyn and Maree cooked dinner. It's almost finished. Come warm up by the fireplace so you can eat."

The spicy aroma of Mexican Cheese Soup — one of Max's favorites — and the crackle of wood popping in the fire greeted them.

———

*P*oor M'Kenzee…usually so in control, but Bren's love box throws her for a loop. Luckily, she's surrounded by family, home, and comfort foods — including this hearty and filling winter soup — when her life gets a bit topsy-turvy!

*I*n the real world, my boys are all about meat and potatoes, not "delicate meals like soup" (or so they claim). Imagine their surprise when they first tasted this recipe. With spicy ground beef, a variety of beans, and plenty of cheese, they adore this soup and ask for it as soon as the temperature drops each fall. Have no fear trying it on your pickiest eaters, too.

INGREDIENTS

1 POUND-BLOCK VELVEETA®, CUBED

1 POUND GROUND BEEF, BROWNED

1 CAN WHOLE KERNEL CORN, UNDRAINED

1 CAN KIDNEY BEANS, UNDRAINED

1 CAN STEWED TOMATOES, UNDRAINED

1 CAN DICED TOMATOES WITH GREEN CHILIES

1 ENVELOPE TACO SEASONING

1 JALAPEÑO PEPPER (OPTIONAL)

NON-STICK COOKING SPRAY

SOUR CREAM

CRUMBLED TORTILLA CHIPS

SHREDDED MEXICAN BLEND CHEESE

INSTRUCTIONS

1. Coat inside of a slow-cooker with non-stick cooking spray.
2. Combine all ingredients into the slow-cooker.
3. Stir mixture.
4. Cover and cook on LOW for 4–5 hours OR cook on HIGH for 3 hours.
5. Serve with a dollop of sour cream and a sprinkling of tortilla chips and shredded cheese.

BEEF & RED MEAT

Remember the old "Where's the beef?" commercials for Wendy's®? Well, it's on our dinner table. Beef and red meat are a staple at our house and most definitely my family's favorite food group! They could happily eat some form of beef every single night. Here are four of our favorites…

EASY LAYERED LASAGNA

Book 4: Take a Chance on Love
Chapter 23

"Davis, I appreciate your offer," the too-smart-for-his-own-good eight-year-old boy declared. "But I think I might go with Landry on the homework help. It sounds like she's got a lot of good experience."

Zane's gentle letdown had Davis doubling over in laughter. "Z Man, I don't blame you one bit," he hooted. "And when Miss Smarty Pants can't figure something out, you just let me know. I'm always here for you, kiddo."

Davis wiped away tears of laughter as he walked to check whatever he'd placed in the oven to heat. Landry wanted to be offended, but she couldn't stave off their good humor and joined them instead.

"What's in the oven?" she asked, glancing at the clock on the microwave in hopes she still had time to eat with the boys before she needed to leave.

"Lasagna," both boys answered with gusto.

"Frozen?"

"Of course not," Davis rebuked.

"Ja-mère made it before she left," Zane provided.

"Ah, now that sounds more like it," Landry said, shooting a coy look at Davis.

If you play with fire — with a fireman — are you bound to get burned?

———

The hallmark of a sweet small town is the community's response when one of their own is in need. Green Hills meets and exceeds that criteria, stepping up time and again to support and provide for one another.

Throughout Book 4, we see examples of that as Landry and Davis must rely on friends and family to accomplish their own quest to take care of Zane and Eddie.

One of many meals they enjoy is Jacqueline's lasagna. With a few "cheat codes" in the form of canned spaghetti sauce and store-bought grated cheese, this recipe turns a traditionally labor-intensive dish into a quick and easy one.

If the batch makes too much for your family, split the lasagna into two 8" x 8" pans: a ceramic or decorative one to serve hot out of the oven, and a foil pan to freeze half before baking. Then you'll have it ready to gift someone a nice dinner when they could use a helping hand.

Simply add the baking instructions to a card of encouragement. Grab a paper shopping bag, set the frozen lasagna in the bottom, toss in a bag of frozen green beans, frozen garlic toast, a tub of brownie bites from the bakery section of the grocery story, and a clamshell of fresh fruit from the produce department. Tie your card on the handles with a pretty ribbon, and *voilá*, a bake-or-save dinner is ready for delivery.

INGREDIENTS

16 OUNCES LASAGNA NOODLES,
BOILED PER INSTRUCTIONS
2 POUNDS LEAN GROUND BEEF, BROWNED
1 TEASPOON ITALIAN SEASONING, MIXED WITH MEAT
2, 24-OUNCE JARS SPAGHETTI SAUCE
16 OUNCES WHOLE MILK RICOTTA CHEESE
16 OUNCES SHREDDED MOZZARELLA CHEESE
8 OUNCES GRATED PARMESAN CHEESE
OLIVE OIL (SPRAY OR LIQUID)

INSTRUCTIONS

1. SPRAY OR DRIZZLE A VERY SMALL AMOUNT OF OLIVE OIL IN A LARGE BAKING DISH. SPREAD IT TO COAT THE BOTTOM AND SIDES OF THE DISH.
2. POUR 1/2 JAR OF SPAGHETTI SAUCE IN THE BOTTOM OF THE DISH.
3. CREATE A SINGLE LAYER OF COOKED LASAGNA NOODLES ON THE SAUCE.
4. SPREAD 1/3 OF THE SEASONED AND BROWNED BEEF EVENLY ACROSS THE NOODLES.
5. DROP SPOONFULS OF RICOTTA CHEESE ACROSS THE GROUND BEEF.
6. POUR 1/2 JAR OF SPAGHETTI SAUCE OVER THE RICOTTA.

7. Layer 4 ounces shredded mozzarella over the sauce.
8. Repeat steps 3–7 two more times for a total of three noodle/meat/sauce/cheese layers.
9. Sprinkle grated parmesan across the top.
10. Bake at 350°F for 25-30 minutes or until sauce is bubbly and cheese is melted.

STEAK ON THE GRILL

Book 2: In the Trenches
Chapter 9

"Janie Lyn, your new, old quilt is fabulous! I've never seen an antique quilt in such pristine condition. I'm leaving it with you and heading to the Get'n'Go." Maree plopped her half of the heavy quilt into Max's hands as she spoke. "We'll have the steaks ready at seven thirty, but y'all come over whenever you — and that fresh bread — are ready. Rhys can even open another jar of my strawberry jam to celebrate... If I don't ration him, he goes through it faster than I'm able to make it!"

"What are we celebrating?" Max asked, sounding a little shell-shocked by Maree's exuberance and the whirlwind of motion she'd created.

"Why, family, friends, and love, of course..."

*J*ust like my family, the Davenports often turn to steaks on the grill when they have time together. In both worlds, nothing beats a well-seasoned, juicy steak, hot off the grill!

Now that the steaks are cooking, let's talk quilts, like Janie Lyn's in the scene above…

*Q*uilting is more than a hobby or craft for me; it's a creative outlet, a source of peace and therapy, and the platform for my role in the fight to end Alzheimer's disease.

When I decided to write wholesome romance, I knew I had to include quilts, quilters, and quilting in every book. Mine is a unique style of quilt fiction, and I'm excited to continue researching and designing quilts for the books!

INGREDIENTS

10–12 OUNCES RIBEYE STEAK, MEDIUM MARBLING

SALT & PEPPER

PERINI RANCH STEAK RUB®

WORCESTERSHIRE SAUCE

INSTRUCTIONS

1. SPRINKLE SALT, PEPPER, AND PERINI® RUB ON ONE SIDE OF THE STEAK.
2. RUB THE SEASONING INTO THE BEEF.
3. USE FORK TINES TO TENDERIZE THE MEAT AND ALLOW SEASONING TO SINK IN.
4. POUR A FEW SHAKES OF WORCESTERSHIRE SAUCE OVER THE SEASONED MEAT.
5. CONTINUE TO RUB THE MARINADE INTO THE MEAT, USING THE FORK TO HELP SAUCE SOAK INTO THE STEAK.
6. REPEAT ON THE OTHER SIDE.
7. COVER AND LET STAND WHILE GRILL HEATS TO 400°F.
8. SET STEAK ON HEATED GRILL FOR 5–6 MINUTES, KEEPING LID CLOSED.
9. FLIP STEAK AND CONTINUE COOKING TO DESIRED DONENESS.
10. REMOVE FROM HEAT.
11. COVER WITH FOIL AND ALLOW STEAK TO SIT FOR 4–5 MINUTES WHILE JUICES SETTLE INTO THE MEAT BEFORE SERVING.

POT ROAST WITH CARROTS, POTATOES, AND ONIONS

Book 1: Grocery Girl
Chapter 6

"I feel like I'm always thanking you for a fantastic meal," Rhys commented as she walked him toward his truck at the end of the night.

"Then there's no reason to stop while you're on a roll. Come to church with us in the morning and indulge in lunch… It's Sunday pot roast, carrots, potatoes, onions, and gravy, with homemade biscuits and more of the strawberry jam that I used on tonight's cake."

"You are the definition of temptation, Maree Davenport," he chided, trying to keep things light and easy. "And you're very persuasive. I'd love to come. Which church, and what time in the morning?"

She gave him all the details as he climbed in the truck, turned on the ignition, and rolled down the driver's-side window.

She stood on the running board to be eye-level with him and, figuring he could ask for forgiveness at church in the morning, he prayed that she'd lean in and end the night with a kiss.

That's when she lowered a hammer to his heart with the softest, kindest words he'd ever been told, "Rhys, I hope that I'm with you again the next time your nightmares hit."

———

This scene is all about Maree chipping away at the walls around Rhys's heart, but don't lose sight of the Sunday dinner she describes. Just like Rhys, it's a keeper!

INGREDIENTS

3 TABLESPOONS OIL

3–4 TABLESPOONS ALL-PURPOSE FLOUR

3-POUND CHUCK ROAST

SALT & PEPPER

2 TABLESPOONS WORCESTERSHIRE SAUCE

2 TABLESPOONS COCONUT AMINOS

1 TABLESPOON MINCED GARLIC

1 CUP WATER OR BEEF BROTH

2 POUNDS POTATOES, PEELED AND CHOPPED

1 POUND CARROTS, PEELED AND CUT INTO CHUNKS

1 WHITE ONION, SLICED INTO RINGS

½ TEASPOON SEASONED SALT

½ TEASPOON DILL WEED

½ TEASPOON CELERY SALT

(OR ADD 2 STALKS CELERY, CUT INTO SMALL PIECES)

ADDITIONAL ¼ CUP ALL-PURPOSE FLOUR FOR GRAVY

2 CUPS WATER OR BEEF BROTH FOR GRAVY

INSTRUCTIONS

1. COAT THE ROAST IN FLOUR.
2. HEAT OIL IN A DUTCH OVEN OR LARGE POT.
3. WHEN OIL IS HOT (BUT NOT SMOKING), ADD ROAST AND BROWN ON ALL SIDES UNTIL BREADING IS STARTING TO CRISP.
4. SCRAPE THE FRIED BITS FROM THE BOTTOM, BUT LEAVE IN THE POT TO SEASON THE VEGETABLES, AND SET ROAST FLAT IN THE POT.
5. ADD WORCESTERSHIRE SAUCE, COCONUT AMINOS, GARLIC, AND WATER.
6. COVER AND BAKE AT 325°F FOR 1 HOUR.
7. ADD VEGETABLES AND SEASONING TO THE POT.
8. COVER AND BAKE AT 325°F FOR AN ADDITIONAL HOUR OR UNTIL CARROTS AND POTATOES ARE SOFT AND MEAT IS TENDER.
9. REMOVE ROAST AND VEGETABLES FROM THE POT.
10. IF DESIRED, STRAIN BROWNED AND FRIED BITS FROM LEFTOVER JUICES. (I USUALLY LEAVE THEM IN THE GRAVY.)
11. ADD ADDITIONAL FLOUR TO POT AND SET ON COOKTOP OVER MEDIUM HEAT.
12. BROWN THE FLOUR IN THE LEFTOVER GREASE AND BITS UNTIL DEEP BROWN.
13. STIR IN WATER OR BEEF BROTH.
14. CONTINUE STIRRING IN A FIGURE-8 UNTIL GRAVY BUBBLES AND BEGINS TO THICKEN.
15. REMOVE FROM HEAT AND POUR INTO A GRAVY BOAT OR SERVING BOWL.
16. SERVE GRAVY OVER ROAST AND VEGETABLES.

TRIPLE T'S CHEESEBURGER

Book 3: Three Times to Make Sure
Chapter 35

The last picture they came to stood in a place of honor as the inspiration for the project: Duke Malone.

M'Kenzee had captured the candid photo of him looking at Jinx one day when she and Jinx had taken lunch to his grandad.

Jinx had explained to her on their way to the memory care facility that the greasy cheeseburger and curly fries from The Three-Toed Turtle — fondly referred to as Triple T's by the locals — had been Mr. Malone's staple lunch for the better part of forty years. He liked it with onions grilled into the patty, mustard on the top bun and mayo on the bottom, with two slices of cheese under one leaf of lettuce, a flat layer of pickles, and a thick tomato slice on top so that it pressed into the inside of the bun to hold it all in place. So, that was what they'd brought for lunch.

During her time at Memorial Care, M'Kenzee had learned that no two minds riddled with dementia behaved the same. Where one person might retain their ability to walk but not speak, another might be verbal but not mobile. One person might never forget their loved ones, while another person lost the names of their family members early in their diagnosis. There was no rhyme or reason as to what one held on to and what one did not.

Mr. Duke Malone had not yet lost his love of a Triple T's cheeseburger.

Just as I had to include quilts, quilters, and quilting in my romance novels, I couldn't create contemporary love stories without weaving in threads of families facing Alzheimer's disease or a dementia diagnosis.

Having lost cherished loved ones on both my side and my husband's side of our family, we are passionate and outspoken about creating a world without Alzheimer's disease. Sharing the heartbreak and devastation families experience throughout the journey of a loved one with Alzheimer's disease or dementia is important, particularly in starting conversations which lead to advocacy. That advocacy leads to funding. Funding leads to research, and research leads to treatments. Access to those treatments will someday lead to a cure. We *will* solve this puzzle. A woman of faith, I believe we ***will*** end ALZ.

Creating engaging characters, sharing their frustrations, and highlighting their beauty amidst Alzheimer's disease — along with my Quilt 2 End ALZ mission — are but a drop in the bucket of what success requires. But it's a drop that isn't there otherwise, and I pray my fictional families bring tangible encouragement to someone who relates to their trials and tribulations in the all-too-real world.

On that note, here is Duke's favorite cheeseburger, just as he remembers…

<u>INGREDIENTS</u>
48 OUNCES 80/20 GROUND BEEF
1 MEDIUM WHITE ONION, DICED
SALT & PEPPER
16 SLICES AMERICAN CHEESE
8 HAMBURGER BUNS
MUSTARD
MAYONAISE
8 SHEETS LEAF LETTUCE
BREAD & BUTTER PICKLES
8 SLICES TOMATO

<u>INSTRUCTIONS</u>

1. MIX GROUND BEEF AND DICED ONIONS IN A BOWL.
2. DIVIDE GROUND BEEF MIXTURE INTO 8 EQUAL PARTS; SHAPE EACH PORTION INTO A 1"-THICK PATTY.
3. SPRINKLE SALT AND PEPPER ON THE TOP OF EACH PATTY.
4. GRILL PATTIES OVER HIGH HEAT FOR 3 MINUTES.
5. FLIP PATTIES; SPRINKLE SALT AND PEPPER ON SECOND SIDE.
6. CONTINUE COOKING OVER HIGH HEAT TO DESIRED DONENESS, ADDING TWO SLICES OF CHEESE TO EACH PATTY FOR THE FINAL MINUTE OF GRILLING.
7. PREP BUNS WHILE PATTIES ARE COOKING BY SPREADING MUSTARD INSIDE THE BOTTOM OF EACH BUN AND MAYONNAISE INSIDE THE TOP OF EACH BUN.
8. REMOVE PATTIES FROM GRILL WHEN READY AND SET ONE ON EACH BUN.
9. LAYER LETTUCE, PICKLES, AND A SLICE OF TOMATO ON TOP OF THE PATTY.
10. CLOSE WITH TOP OF BUN AND SERVE WHILE HAMBURGER PATTY IS HOT.

WHITE MEAT & FISH

When you fish for love,
bait with your heart, not your brain.
Mark Twain

As Coach and I age, I try to incorporate more and more white meat and fish into our meals. I've enjoyed experimenting with techniques, types of fish, and seasonings. In the end, what I've found is that simple is best. Salt, pepper, and a splash lemon juice are really all a great piece of fish needs to be juicy, flaky, and fabulous.

Chicken is another story. I'm as likely to grill it with little more than seasoned salt and barbecue sauce as I am to dress it up in an elaborate casserole. It's hard to mess up chicken, and for that I am quite thankful! Either way, these four recipes are ones we enjoy time and again.

GRAM'S CHICKEN & DORITOS®

Book 2: In the Trenches
Chapter 24

Laughing at herself and how quickly she'd gotten caught up in her fantasy, Janie Lyn refocused on the chicken casserole she planned to make for their dinner. A simple recipe Gram had made on a regular basis when Janie Lyn was growing up, she didn't need Maxwell to test the flavors — she knew it was fail-safe — but she'd developed a hankering for it when she'd typed it up that morning. They had all the ingredients to make it except one: nacho-cheese-flavored tortilla chips.

Make it without the chips or run to the store?

Run to the store??

A quiver snaked through Janie Lyn's stomach. A chill ran down her spine.

———

The chicken casserole that Janie Lyn's Gram taught her to make is actually my mother-in-law's Chicken & Doritos® recipe.

It's what I take to families with new babies most often, and it's a huge hit at tailgates!

Plain, corn Doritos® are more difficult to find than they used to be, so you might have to substitute another brand of corn tortilla chips. If so, I recommend one with thicker chips rather than the thin restaurant style.

Also, the recipe calls for Velveeta® shredded cheese because it's famous for melting better than other brands.

True, the name brands are a little more expensive. *But…* if I can find plain Doritos® and Velveeta® shredded cheese, I think they're worth the splurge and give this casserole a richer flavor.

I serve Chicken & Doritos® with extra chips, buttered corn, and strawberry shortcake for dessert — yum!

INGREDIENTS

10-OUNCE BAG OF PLAIN DORITOS®

24 OUNCES COOKED CHICKEN, CHOPPED

½ SMALL ONION, CHOPPED

2 TABLESPOONS SALTED BUTTER

4½-OUNCE CAN CHOPPED GREEN CHILES

10½-OUNCE CAN CREAM OF CHICKEN SOUP

10½-OUNCE CAN CREAM OF MUSHROOM SOUP

1 CUP CHICKEN BROTH

1 CUP GRATED VELVEETA® CHEESE

INSTRUCTIONS

1. Pour Doritos® into a 10" x 13" pan.
2. Top with chicken.
3. Saute onion in butter over medium heat for 2–3 minutes.
4. Add green chiles, soups, and broth to skillet.
5. Cook over medium heat until mixture begins to boil.
6. Pour mixture over chicken.
7. Top with grated cheese.
8. Bake at 375°F for 20 minutes or until juices bubble and cheese is melted.

NANA'S CHICKEN SPAGHETTI

Book 1: Grocery Girl
Chapter 5

Rhys was exhausted after a very long day. And he was confused by the guy opening what he believed to be Maree's door. Correction: the very big guy with the very big dog opening what he believed to be Maree's door.

"Oh." Rhys stumbled and eyed the dog. "I'm…uh…" His explanation died. He ran a hand through his hair. Looking down, he searched for something to say. He wanted to be mad, but three conversations did not give him any right to — nor any hold over — a beautiful girl.

And he didn't want a hold over anyone. He was stupid to have thought—

"Looking for my sister, I believe," the huge fellow interrupted Rhys's thoughts and finished his sentence for him.

Rhys expelled a relieved sigh. He was grateful that he'd been put out of his misery sooner rather than later. He'd dissect that natural response later.

"Yeah, I'm Rhys Larsen," he offered, putting out his hand to shake.

"Max Davenport." Max shook hands, polite and not quite frowning, but with his overprotective, big brother look still firmly in place. "And this is Hank."

They were standing on the porch with a bright light coming from inside the house, so it had been difficult for Rhys to clearly see his face. Looking closer, Rhys paused, shocked he hadn't recognized the celebrity athlete the second the door had opened.

"Max Davenport," Rhys repeated flatly, the weight of the world suddenly reappearing on his shoulders. "Of course you are." He could only shake his head. That response seemed to be his new norm. Maree was something else, and that something was more magnetic, more interesting, and more captivating at every turn.

"Maree, your fireman's here," Max hollered toward the back of the house as he stepped back to let Rhys in.

As Rhys paused to greet the dog with a soothing scratch behind the ears, Maree poked her head around the living room wall with her cheerful, effervescent smile. Rhys looked up from where he was kneeling in front of Hank, his eyes settling on Maree. Something shifted in his world. An axis righted. The weight lifted.

Rhys was too tired to hide his response to her…couldn't find the energy required to mask it. He figured Max had seen the transformation. He could feel it himself. Rhys also had a sense that he'd just passed a test, one he'd not even been aware of taking.

"Come on in," Maree invited. "I left the chicken spaghetti out for you in case you hadn't eaten. Come back here to the kitchen."

He stood up from petting Hank, nodded his head once to Max to excuse himself, and followed Maree.

Just as he turned into the kitchen, Rhys would've sworn he'd heard Max tell Hank, "That smitten boy is toast." Surely not.

———

This chicken spaghetti might be the world's very best, most effective comfort food.

I got it from Coach's mom, Sandra, when he and I married in 1995. She got it from a church cookbook in the '80s. I'm certain it's been passed around for generations. And while I've seen slight variations of it here and there, this is by far my favorite way to make it.

Need to impress a fireman? This is it.
Need a potluck dish that travels well? This is it.
Need a quick dinner solution? This is it.
Need to feed an entire football team? This is it. (But perhaps triple — or quadruple — it.)

Whatever you need, this recipe is the answer!
I usually serve it with French bread, roasted Brussels sprouts, and MawMaw's Marshmallow Fruit Salad — you'll have to wait until the next Green Hills cookbook for that one.

INGREDIENTS

3 CUPS WATER
10½ OUNCES CHICKEN BROTH
12 OUNCES SPAGHETTI
2 TABLESPOONS SALTED BUTTER
1 WHITE ONION, CHOPPED
1 CUP CELERY, CHOPPED
1 GREEN BELL PEPPER, CHOPPED
4-OUNCE JAR CHOPPED PIMENTOS
24 OUNCES COOKED CHICKEN, CHOPPED
2, 10½-OUNCE CANS CREAM OF MUSHROOM SOUP
8 OUNCES SHREDDED VELVEETA® CHEESE

INSTRUCTIONS

1. COOK SPAGHETTI IN WATER AND BROTH. DRAIN SPAGHETTI AND SET ASIDE.
2. SAUTE ONION, CELERY, AND BELL PEPPER IN BUTTER.
3. STIR SOUP INTO SAUTEED VEGETABLES.
4. ADD PIMENTOS, CHICKEN, AND SPAGHETTI TO SOUP MIXTURE.
5. PLACE IN CASSEROLE DISH.
6. SPRINKLE CHEESE ON TOP.
7. BAKE AT 350°F UNTIL CHEESE MELTS.

PORK CHOP CASSEROLE

Book 3: Three Times to Make Sure
Chapter 24

Landry Stark guided their conversation from defeat to hope with the smooth ease of an ice-skater swishing across the rink. Quite impressive. And brilliant, it seemed. A bubbly bundle of energy, Landry balanced that constant motion with a talent for listening. Patience, Jinx realized; that was her secret superpower. She'd be an incredible doctor — attentive, calm, and caring.

M'Kenzee read from her punch list and notes, explaining the big picture of the remodeling effort, while the rest of the group fixed their plates. Jinx agreed with Landry, the casserole looked — and smelled — too good to not indulge. A thick, buttery gravy covered round roasted potatoes, caramelized onions, tender carrots, and juicy pork chops at least an inch thick and browned to perfection. Jinx's mouth watered, although he would've sworn he wasn't hungry before Miss Sadie and Landry arrived.

———

I admire Landry and M'Kenzee. I respect women who lead with love, give lots of grace — to themselves as well as to others — and don't shy away from opportunities to make their world a better place. I purposefully write these traits and tendencies into my female characters.

Miss Sadie embraces her role as a matriarch in Green Hills; she is patient and kind while displaying strength and wisdom.

Maree loves in a big, all-consuming way; she is jubilant and bubbly while illustrating a keen and brilliant entrepreneurial spirit.

Janie Lyn is quiet and introspective while proving still waters run deep and that honey attracts more flies than vinegar; her discernment and diplomacy impress readers again and again.

M'Kenzee is honest to a fault while expecting people's best effort, starting with herself.

Landry is fun and light-hearted while modeling drive and determination paired with a huge heart and a deep capacity to love.

M ost importantly, the women of Green Hills lift one another up, they celebrate each other's victories, and they find joy in one another's gifts.

The Davenports and their friends look upon each other as sisters-in-arms to build up their community rather than seeing one another as competition to tear down. Having friends and family who love unconditionally — who boost and buoy when needed — empowers every member of the group.

I pray the ladies in my books inspire others to be *that* person...*that* friend, *that* sister, *that* mother, *that* daughter, *that* cousin, or *that* aunt who shines her light on all those blessed by her love in such a way that their world is automatically brighter, happier, lovelier, and more joyful.

INGREDIENTS

2 TABLESPOONS OIL

2 POUNDS PORK LOIN CHOPS

SEASONED SALT AND MRS. DASH®

2 POUNDS POTATOES, CUBED

1 POUND CARROTS, CHOPPED INTO 3" CHUNKS

1 YELLOW ONION, SLICED INTO RINGS

2, 10½-OUNCE CANS CREAM OF MUSHROOM SOUP

INSTRUCTIONS

1. PAN-FRY PORK CHOPS IN OIL UNTIL BROWNED ON BOTH SIDES.
2. PLACE PORK CHOPS IN A LARGE BAKING DISH.
3. SPRINKLE SEASONED SALT AND MRS. DASH® OVER THE MEAT.
4. IN A MICROWAVE-SAFE BOWL, COMBINE POTATOES AND CARROTS WITH WATER. STEAM THEM IN THE MICROWAVE ON HIGH HEAT FOR 3–5 MINUTES TO PRECOOK THEM.
5. DRAIN POTATOES AND CARROTS.
6. COVER MEAT WITH PRECOOKED VEGETABLES AND ONION.
7. SPREAD SOUP OVER THE VEGETABLES.

8. COVER WITH FOIL.
9. BAKE AT 350°F FOR 30 MINUTES OR UNTIL
   VEGETABLES ARE SOFT AND GRAVY BUBBLES.

RICE KRISPIES® CHICKEN

Book 4: Take a Chance on Love
Chapter 33

"I don't know how I feel," he countered.

"Yes." Jacqueline pointed the spatula at him. "You do."

"And how do you know how I feel?" Davis tried to turn the tables on the interrogation.

"Because I know you, SonShine." Daniel Aaron Davis answered to a lot of nicknames; pulling out the one that only his mom used equated to fighting dirty. She knew exactly how to tug on his heartstrings.

"How do I know she's The One? I mean, of course I love her. She's one of my best friends; maybe that's all that is meant to be between us...a fun and flirty friendship. I've tried to have more than that with other girls, and I stink at it. As soon as we get serious, it falls apart." Davis emphasized what he thought of relationships that get serious with theatrical air quotes. "What if she doesn't love me?"

"I'm going to go out on a limb here and guess that the love you feel for Maree Davenport is not the same as the way you feel drawn to Landry."

"I'm willing to concede that point," Davis allowed with a sly smile at his wise and wonderful mom.

"I'd also wager that a fun and flirty friendship, as you put it, is just pretty packaging. From what your dad and I can tell, your relationship with Landry goes well beyond such surface wrapping."

"That's two points in your favor."

"She's worth giving get serious another try." She copied his air quotes. "Besides, all those other girls loved you too much."

"Excuse me? The girlfriends who loved me too much were a bust, but Landry will be The One? Is that because she doesn't love me enough?"

"The girls you've dated in the past loved the thought of you, but you only liked them. That creates a mismatch. A relationship can't work if one person loves the other person more. Landry is The One because you love her just as she loves you; together y'all are balanced."

Jacqueline let that sink in while she took a pan of breaded and baked chicken from the oven.

"Dinner's ready; please go tell Zane and your dad to wash up so we can eat," she instructed.

Still befuddled, Davis turned toward the door to the backyard to do as ordered.

"And SonShine?"

"Yes, ma'am?" Davis looked back over his shoulder.

"That's three points in my favor." Then she winked at him before carrying the serving platters to the table.

"Game, set, match," he said under his breath. "Mom wins again."

———

*B*ook 4 is dedicated to — and Davis's personality is inspired by — my son. Drawing on our relationship made writing the scenes with Davis and Jacqueline a downright blast. I won't lie… Several of those scenes brought tears to my eyes as I wrote.

I particularly appreciate this one where Mom knows best!

*T*he breaded chicken Jacqueline takes out of the oven in the scene is a recipe my mom and I "stole" from one of my childhood bonus moms, my best friend's mother, Sheri.

It begins by soaking chicken breasts in seasoned milk and breading them with crushed Rice Krispies® cereal. The secret to keeping the chicken juicy is to scatter pats of butter across the pan which melt into the chicken while it bakes.

If I've tweaked this one over the years, it was done accidentally, but rest assured… As it's written is quite delicious. And it's incredibly easy to prepare.

My mom always served it with wild rice, broccoli and cheese sauce, cantaloupe, buttery dinner rolls, and Rice Krispies® Treats for dessert, so I do it exactly the same way.

My family never tires of having Rice Krispies® Chicken and is game to have it on the menu every single month!

<u>INGREDIENTS</u>

6 CHICKEN BREASTS

2 GALLON-SIZED ZIPPER BAGGIES

24-OUNCE FAMILY SIZE BOX OF RICE KRISPIES®

(RESERVE 6 CUPS OF CEREAL FOR MAKING TREATS.)

1 CUP WHOLE MILK

1 TEASPOON SALT

1 TEASPOON PEPPER

1 TEASPOON MRS. DASH®

1 TEASPOON SEASONED SALT

1 TEASPOON CELERY SALT

1 TEASPOON ONION POWDER

1 TEASPOON GARLIC POWDER

NONSTICK COOKING SPRAY

1 STICK SALTED BUTTER

<u>INSTRUCTIONS</u>

1. PLACE CHICKEN BREASTS IN A GALLON-SIZED BAGGIE.
2. ADD MILK AND SEASONINGS TO THE BAGGIE.
3. SEAL AND SET IN THE FRIDGE TO SOAK WHILE PREPARING CEREAL.
4. ADD CEREAL TO THE SECOND BAGGIE. SEAL BAGGIE AND LIGHTLY CRUSH CEREAL WITH A ROLLING PIN, A GLASS JAR, OR YOUR HANDS.
5. COAT A CASSEROLE DISH WITH COOKING SPRAY.
6. REMOVE A PIECE OF CHICKEN FROM THE MILK MIXTURE. DROP IT IN THE CEREAL BAGGIE AND SHAKE TO COAT THE MEAT WITH BREADING.
7. SET THE CHICKEN BREAST IN THE BAKING PAN.
8. REPEAT WITH ALL CHICKEN PIECES.

9. THINLY SLICE THE STICK OF BUTTER. SET PATS OF
   BUTTER ON TOP OF THE BREADED CHICKEN.
10. COVER WITH FOIL AND BAKE AT 375°F FOR 30–35
    MINUTES OR UNTIL CHICKEN IS OPAQUE BUT STILL
    JUICY (165°F INTERNAL TEMPERATURE).
11. REMOVE FOIL IN THE FINAL 3–5 MINUTES OF BAKE
    TIME TO TOAST CEREAL IF DESIRED.

VEGGIES & SIDES

Life expectancy would grow by leaps and bounds if green vegetables smelled as good as bacon.
Doug Larson

Please no one tell my husband — who as I mentioned before is all about the meat — that I could quite easily be a vegetarian. I love fruits, vegetables, salads, side dishes, and casseroles.

I'm the one regularly ordering the 5-side platter at a restaurant or stealing raw veggies from the fridge. And although I tend to invent new creations that turn into favorites using random ingredients I find in the kitchen, I have accrued an extensive collection of delicious recipes for veggies and sides.

To limit myself, I've chosen one from each book to share. I'm eager to hear what you think!

AUNT T'S TACO SALAD

Book 1: Grocery Girl
Chapter 22

Rhys came back to the kitchen his usual calm self. He was wearing another pair of well-worn jeans, a Texas Rangers t-shirt to nettle Maree about her Houston Astros (who'd gone on to win while she slept earlier), and nothing on his feet. His dark blond hair was damp, and the waves seemed to beg for her touch. When he stopped in front of her for a chaste kiss and a wink, she grinned into his gaze and reached her hand up for a quick run of her fingers through his hair.

"Here we go again," Sadie muttered with a shake of her head. But when Rhys walked right up to Sadie and planted a kiss on her cheek, too, the older woman blushed like a schoolgirl.

"Miss Sadie, how can I help?" he asked as if nothing odd or unusual had occurred.

"Set the table, please," she instructed, reclaiming her composure. Just as he

was grinning and winking at Maree once more, Sadie added, "And set it for four; I told Daniel to come back for supper."

Rhys rolled his eyes in pretend exasperation. "Who's Daniel?" Maree asked, which caused Rhys to laugh outright. The laughter proved to be almost as therapeutic as the running and the kissing, not to mention the retching that was tossed in there, too. The tears — the first ones he'd shed in over ten years — had still not registered. Yet.

———

Can't you envision Miss Sadie fussing over dinner while Rhys is fussing over Maree?

I see Miss Sadie chopping and tossing the taco salad with busy hands right up until the moment Rhys kisses her cheek. Then, she'd have to slow down, pause, and enjoy the blush that heats her cheek.

Miss Sadie maintains a crucial presence in Green Hills… She provides a voice of reason, wisdom from a lifetime of experience, and encouragement when one needs it the most. Her welcoming way of guiding without judging comes from my Mema, the most inclusive and understanding person I've ever known. When I'm writing scenes with Miss Sadie, I feel Mema's presence in my heart and in my soul.

This taco salad recipe comes from another family member who demonstrates love for all, no matter their successes or their stumbles. My Aunt Teresa believes in everyone — sees the good in everyone.

That's a trait I strive to replicate…just like her incredible taco salad!

<u>INGREDIENTS</u>

1 HEAD OF LETTUCE, WASHED, DRIED, AND TORN INTO SALAD
PIECES
1 MEDIUM CAN OF RANCH STYLE® BEANS, RINSED AND DRAINED
1 PINT CHERRY OR GRAPE TOMATOES, WASHED AND CUT IN HALF
1 BUNCH GREEN ONIONS, CHOPPED
SMALL BOTTLE CATALINA DRESSING
1 CUP MEXICAN BLEND SHREDDED CHEESE
1 BAG NACHO CHEESE DORITOS®

<u>INSTRUCTIONS</u>

1. PREPARE VEGGIES AS MENTIONED ABOVE. DRY
   EVERYTHING WELL SO THE LEFTOVERS LAST LONGER
   — NO ONE LIKES SOGGY SALAD!
2. IN A LARGE BOWL, COMBINE LETTUCE, BEANS,
   TOMATO, AND ONIONS.
3. DRIZZLE A LITTLE CATALINA DRESSING OVER THE
   VEGGIES AND MIX WELL. ADD MORE CATALINA IN
   SMALL AMOUNTS UNTIL THE SALAD IS COATED, BUT
   NOT DRENCHED.
4. STIR IN CHEESE.
5. JUST BEFORE SERVING, STIR IN A COUPLE HANDFULS
   OF DORITOS®. I LIKE TO PUT THE REST OF THE
   CHIPS IN A BASKET ON THE TABLE... THEY ARE
   PERFECT FOR HELPING SCOOP SALAD ON A FORK.

BROCCOLI SALAD

Book 3: Three Times to Make Sure
Chapter 9

Audrie Boucher, owner of the yoga studio at Daisy Lake that Maree liked to drag everyone to on a weekly basis, had offered to coordinate the nondessert, nonmeat items. She'd sent out a text to their Saturday morning classmates, and the masses had answered her call. Broccoli salad, potato salad, green salad, relish trays, fruit trays, cheese trays, baskets of crackers and crisps, and dishes of vegetable sides created a twenty-foot buffet. Again, a staggering response to support her family.

———

Long before I decided to write down the love stories that live in my head, I had an idea for a romance involving a yoga instructor. I've known her backstory, her obstacles, and her personality for years so she's very real to me.

In some ways, she's my first Green Hills character, and in fact, she's part of all four books in *The Davenports* miniseries.

Like most of our Green Hills friends, she's an overcomer. Her journey has not been easy, but she's a survivor…a warrior. I'm both eager and anxious to share her journey to finding her soulmate, but if anyone deserves a deep and abiding love that lasts forever, Audrie is our girl.

Fingers crossed, we can look for her book to release in the spring of 2026. By then, we'll have returned home from *The Green Hills of Scotland* miniseries and experienced a fun and quirky holiday with my second novella in *The Christmas Collection*.

In the meantime, we'll continue to see Audrie's cameo appearances, giving readers a glimpse of what's to come.

<u>SALAD INGREDIENTS</u>

6 CUPS BROCCOLI, CHOPPED

1 CUP SHARP CHEDDAR CHEESE, THICKLY GRATED

½ CUP DRIED CRANBERRIES

½ CUP RAISINS

½ CUP SALTED SUNFLOWER SEEDS

½ CUP BACON, COOKED AND CRUMBLED

(ABOUT 5–6 STRIPS)

¼ CUP RED ONION, DICED

<u>DRESSING INGREDIENTS</u>

1 CUP OLIVE OIL MAYONNAISE

¼ CUP SUGAR

1 TABLESPOON WHITE WINE VINEGAR

SALT & PEPPER

INSTRUCTIONS

1. WHISK DRESSING INGREDIENTS TOGETHER IN A LARGE SERVING BOWL.
2. ADD SALAD INGREDIENTS AND TOSS TO DISPERSE THE DRESSING EVENLY.
3. CHILL FOR ONE HOUR AND SERVE COLD.

CORN PUDDING

Book 2: In the Trenches
Chapter 9

Dinner was spectacular. Max was grateful to be there, glad he'd run home instead of burrowing in his town house in Kansas City to avoid the public for the three days of the long weekend he had off of practice and meetings.

Rhys cooked the steaks to perfection; seared with a robust seasoning rub on the outside and pink throughout, each bite melted in Max's mouth. Maree had made his favorite corn pudding and her famous "smash" potatoes on the side. Janie Lyn's colorful salad was crisp and flavorful, served with a tangy honey mustard dressing. And of course, their homemade bread stole the show. Topped with butter and jam, it tasted divine.

After dinner, they pulled their chairs around the fire pit in the center of Rhys's backyard. The Oklahoma sunset painted a breathtaking masterpiece with burning shades of red and orange that faded into feathers of gold and pink extending the length of the horizon. When the day relinquished its hold, the clear night sky created a deep midnight-navy backdrop for a billion stars twinkling bright.

———

"*D*inner was spectacular" is a common sentiment in Green Hills.

I figure if I'm going to create a fictional town from my imagination, I might as well make sure the folks there eat really, really well!

*T*his corn pudding recipe is a good example. A game-changer, your team will love it as much as Maxwell does in Book 2.

The best part about it? Basically, it requires one pot and one step of instructions...

INGREDIENTS

1 BAG FROZEN CORN (10–12 OUNCES)

2, 11-OUNCE CANS GREEN GIANT MEXICORN®

14.75-OUNCE CAN CREAM STYLE CORN

8.5-OUNCE BOX JIFFY® CORN MUFFIN MIX

½ BLOCK CREAM CHEESE (4 OUNCES)

¾ CUP WATER

¼ CUP SALTED BUTTER

DASHES OF SALT, PEPPER, AND SEASONED SALT

INSTRUCTIONS

1. Combine all ingredients in a slow cooker.
2. Set temperature to low, cover, and cook.
3. Stir after an hour.
4. Cook on low another 2-3 hours or until edges are browning and the pudding has a soft, pillowy texture.

SQUASH & POTATO HASH

Book 4: Take a Chance on Love
Chapter 33

"Someone's in an awfully good mood," Jacqueline Davis laughed, trying to keep her feet underneath her legs as her youngest child swung her around the kitchen in a frolicking jig. "Should I try to guess what — or who — is behind it?"

"Is it that obvious?" Davis asked his mom, setting her back in front of the cooktop in his kitchen from where he'd snatched her. He made sure she'd regained her balance, performed a proper bow, and kissed her cheek before sniffing out the vegetables pan-frying in a cast-iron skillet. "Squash and potato hash... Yum!"

In order to share this recipe, I had to devise a list of ingredients and measurements... When writing a cookbook, it's what one does.

The truth of this recipe, however, is that whatever squash you have on hand — zucchini, yellow, butternut, acorn, spaghetti, any type really — and whatever potatoes you have on hand — russet, red, fingerling, gold, red, purple, or sweet — are perfect to use, and the amounts honestly don't matter one bit.

Simply fill a cast-iron skillet with chopped "whatevers" you find in the kitchen, stir in some oil, and sprinkle salt, pepper, and sugar over the veggies as they pan-fry. Let them cook until the hash is so soft, it's starting to fall apart. And be sure to let a layer caramelize to get plenty of crispy, crunchy bits, which are the best part.

INGREDIENTS

3 POUNDS POTATOES

2 ZUCCHINI SQUASH

2 YELLOW SQUASH

1 YELLOW ONION

3–4 TABLESPOONS OIL

$\frac{1}{4}$ CUP SUGAR

$\frac{1}{2}$ TEASPOON SALT

$\frac{1}{2}$ TEASPOON PEPPER

INSTRUCTIONS

1. WASH AND CHOP THE VEGETABLES.
2. COMBINE CHOPPED VEGGIES, OIL, SUGAR, SALT, AND PEPPER IN A CAST-IRON SKILLET. STIR WELL TO COAT THE VEGGIES WITH OIL AND SEASONING.

3. PAN-FRY OVER MEDIUM-HIGH HEAT FOR 25-30 MINUTES, DEPENDING ON DESIRED DONENESS. NOTE: STIR HASH OCCASIONALLY AND NEVER LEAVE FRYING PAN UNATTENDED WITH HOT OIL.
4. SERVE HOT FROM THE PAN.

SWEET TREATS

***Desserts are the fairy tales of the kitchen—
a happily-ever-after to supper.
Terri Guillemets***

If ever I need proof that I'm weak and undisciplined, I only have to glance at a dessert menu, sniff chocolate in the air, or scroll through my Instagram feed. In no time flat, I'm scrounging the house for a sweet treat.

Not only do I love indulging in dessert, I also find great joy and relaxation in baking and experimenting with sweet recipes. Here are a few that appear with happily-ever-afters in *The Davenports…*

APRICOT FRIED PIES

Book 2: In the Trenches
Chapter 12

"Can I help?" he asked as he began washing his hands.

"Um. Uh, yes. Sure." Her voice quivered. He liked it. He liked ruffling her feathers. "You can stir the fruit in that pot on the stove."

"What's in here with the apricots?" he asked as he started to stir the mixture. Food — talking about it, preparing it, sharing it — settled her. While he was relieved she felt the electrical charge between them, he didn't want to make her nervous or skittish.

"Apricots, raisins, dried cranberries, a little lemon juice, sugar, and butter." Sugahh and butahh. His heart flipped. "Let an apricot cool a bit on the spoon. Then you can test it to see if it's soft enough. And sweet enough." She was killing him.

———

When I'm asked to describe the heat level in my Green Hills romance novels I explain there is a lot of sizzle but no sex.

The apricot fried pie scene in Book 2 perfectly illustrates what I mean: tons of tension and chemistry, yet only one small and innocent kiss which Maxwell places on Janie Lyn's forehead in kind reassurance. So fun to write…and I pray a ton of fun to read as well!

Growing up in a small Texas town, homemade fried pies were a regular treat. My Grandma Syble (the Virginia portion of my pen name) made an amazing apricot version. When Janie Lyn — flustered over Maxwell — needed something grand but easy to make, this recipe came to mind as the perfect fit.

CRUST INGREDIENTS

3 CUPS ALL-PURPOSE FLOUR

1½ CUPS VEGETABLE SHORTENING, KEPT COLD

1 TEASPOON SALT

6–10 TABLESPOONS WHOLE MILK, KEPT COLD

<u>FILLING INGREDIENTS</u>

5 POUNDS FRESH APRICOTS, PITTED AND QUARTERED
½ CUP RAISINS
½ CUP DRIED CRANBERRIES
1 CUP GRANULATED SUGAR
1 CUP BROWN SUGAR
½ CUP ALL-PURPOSE FLOUR
¼ CUP LEMON JUICE
2 TABLESPOONS SALTED BUTTER

<u>TOPPING INGREDIENTS</u>

1 EGG
2 TABLESPOONS WATER
EXTRA GRANULATED SUGAR AND GROUND CINNAMON

<u>INSTRUCTIONS</u>

1. FORM PIE CRUST. BEGIN BY SIFTING FLOUR AND SALT TOGETHER.
2. CUT IN COLD SHORTENING USING A PASTRY CUTTER OR FORK TO KEEP THE SHORTENING COLD. CONTINUE CUTTING CHUNKS OF SHORTENING IN UNTIL THEY ARE PEA-SIZED.
3. ADD COLD MILK 1 TABLESPOON AT A TIME UNTIL DOUGH FORMS A SMOOTH, ROUND BALL. IT SHOULD HOLD TOGETHER AND NOT BE STICKY.
4. FLATTEN DOUGH INTO A ROUND DISK, COVER WITH PLASTIC WRAP, AND CHILL IN THE REFRIGERATOR FOR AT LEAST 30 MINUTES.
5. WHILE DOUGH IS CHILLING, PREPARE FILLING.

6. Combine all filling ingredients in a stock pot or dutch oven.

7. Stir well until mixture begins to look juicy.

8. Place pot over medium heat and cook until mixture begins to thicken.

9. Remove from heat and set aside.

10. When dough is finished chilling, roll dough into a large rectangle on a lightly floured workspace.

11. Using an ice cream scooper, set mounds of pie filling on one half of the dough rectangle, spacing the mounds two inches apart from one another.

12. Gently work your hands under the empty half of the dough rectangle and flip it over the fruit filling mounds. Press the dough together between the mounds to seal each mini pie.

13. In a small measuring glass, beat the egg and water together to make an egg wash. Pour it over the dough rectangle, smoothing it evenly with your hands or a pastry brush.

14. Sprinkle granulated sugar and cinnamon across the top of the dough rectangle.

15. Using a rolling pastry cutter or a sharp knife, cut along the fused lines of dough to create small rectangular pies.

16. Place the mini pies on a lined cookie sheet or jelly roll pan, leaving a small space between them. Check to see that the seams remain fused so the fruit filling doesn't escape while cooking.

17. Using the tip of a sharp knife, cut a small vent for steam to escape the top of each pie.

18. Using a deep fryer or skillet, fry the pies in oil over medium-high heat (OR bake the pies at 425°F for 15–20 minutes) until crust is golden brown. (Never walk away from the hot grease.)

19. Set cooked pies on a cooling rack for a few minutes before serving. Caution: FILLING IS VERY HOT!

BROOKIES

Book 4: Take a Chance on Love
Chapter 18

"Are we waxing, or are we waning?" Davis asked from where he stood behind their chairs.

They both jumped a mile high, as if he'd caught them up to no good instead of dutifully studying earth science.

"The better question is, what are you doing frightening us half to death? Can't you make a little noise before you walk up on someone?" Landry accused.

"I'm not waxing or waning. I'm full, maybe about to pop," Zane whined. The unusual despondency in his voice put Davis on high alert. "My brain is full, stuffed with words I can't remember and pictures that don't make sense. Can I quit?"

Landry flashed Davis a worried look. He wasn't alone in his concern.

School from home didn't officially begin until Monday, and Zane had already hit his threshold for self-paced learning. Yikes.

"Quit is a pretty strong word, Z Man. I've known you a very long time — eight full years — and I've known your dad even longer than that. I've never known the Cadell men to believe in quitting. What if we pause instead?"

"How long does a pause last?" Zane asked, at least a little interested in Davis's idea.

"I'd say at least long enough to throw on some sweats, load up in the truck, swing through the drive-through at Fish & Spoon to pick up dinner and a few brookies with ice cream on top, and drive out to Daisy Lake to watch the sun set over the water while we eat our dinner."

The Davenports eat well in Green Hills! And we know from multiple occurrences throughout Books 1–4 that brookies — Fish & Spoon's famous chocolate chip cookie sandwiched between two layers of brownie and topped with toasted almonds, caramel, and crunchy granules of coarse sea salt — are a fan favorite.

The scene above reminds readers that a pause and a "brookie break" are good for the mind and for the soul. Keep your eyes open for them in various Green Hills novels.

Personally, I could have brookies for breakfast, lunch, and dinner… They are that good. When you make them for your loved ones, please let me know what they think, too!

CHOCOLATE CHIP COOKIE DOUGH INGREDIENTS

2¼ CUPS ALL-PURPOSE FLOUR

1 TEASPOON BAKING SODA

1 TEASPOON SALT

¼ CUP ALL-VEGETABLE SHORTENING

⅓ CUP SALTED BUTTER, SOFTENED

¾ CUP GRANULATED SUGAR

¾ CUP BROWN SUGAR

1 TEASPOON VANILLA EXTRACT

2 EGGS

1½ CUPS SEMI-SWEET CHOCOLATE CHIPS

BROWNIE BATTER

1 CUP SUGAR

½ CUP ALL-PURPOSE FLOUR

½ CUP COCOA

¼ TEASPOON SALT

¼ TEASPOON BAKING POWDER

2 EGGS

½ CUP OIL

1 TEASPOON VANILLA

TOPPING INGREDIENTS

⅓ CUP CARAMEL ICE CREAM SAUCE

COURSE SEA SALT

10-OUNCE BAG OF PECAN HALVES

INSTRUCTIONS

1. Grease a 9" x 13" baking dish and set aside.
2. Mix chocolate chip cookie dough. Start by combining the flour, baking soda, and salt in a small bowl with a spoon.
3. In a mixer, beat together the shortening, butter, granulated sugar, brown sugar, vanilla, and eggs until well-blended.
4. Stir in the flour mixture.
5. Add the chocolate chips and mix just until spread evenly throughout the dough. Set aside.
6. Mix brownie batter by combining all brownie batter ingredients in a large bowl. Stir just until moist throughout. Split the batter evenly into two bowls.
7. Pour one bowl of brownie batter (half the full mixture) into the greased baking dish.
8. Gently drop the chocolate chip cookie dough on top of the brownie batter and smooth slowly until dough is flat.
9. Pour the second bowl of brownie batter on top of the cookie dough.
10. Drizzle caramel sauce over brownie batter in a zig-zag pattern. Using the tip of a spoon or butter knife, drag through the ribbon of caramel to swirl it on top of the brownie batter.
11. Sprinkle course sea salt over the batter and caramel.
12. Place pecan halves in neat columns and rows on top of the batter and caramel. Leave two

INCHES BETWEEN PECAN HALVES; THIS CREATES CUT
LINES TO SERVE YOUR BROOKIES.

13. BAKE AT 350°F FOR 20-25 MINUTES OR UNTIL A
TOOTHPICK COMES OUT CLEAN FROM THE CENTER OF
THE PAN.

14. SERVE ALONE OR WITH VANILLA ICE CREAM, FRESH
FRUIT, OR WHIPPED TOPPING FOR EXTRA
AWESOMENESS.

CHOCOLATE CHIP COOKIES

Book 3: Three Times to Make Sure
Chapter 19

"Ready for a late lunch?" Janie Lyn ducked her head into the upstairs theater room M'Kenzee had been inhabiting for hours.

"Sure, I'll be right down."

"No need — I brought it up." Janie Lyn came through the doorway with a large tray in her arms. Glasses of sweet tea, dessert napkins with a large homemade chocolate chip cookie on top of each, two cloth napkins, two forks, and two plates piled with grilled cheese sandwiches, chips, and fruit salad took up every inch of the tray.

"My goodness," M'Kenzee exclaimed, hopping up and setting Bren's note-book aside so she could help with the heavy load. "That's more than lunch; it's a feast."

———

*G*reen Hills novels are more than formulaic romance. Woven throughout the stories are threads of loving families, a caring community, courage and faith, quilts and quilters, examples of dementia and Alzheimer's disease, yoga and sports, books, and food…lots of food.

The scene above depicts friendship and sisterhood, two other themes common in my writing. It also mentions the chocolate chip cookies Janie Lyn bakes in preparation for Christmas, a dressed up version of a classic.

Nestled in among holiday cakes and pies, our family loves a tin of cookies. Without fail, the cookies are one of the first sweet treats to go. We are all guilty of grabbing a cookie each time we walk by the dessert table…

They simply taste too good to pass up!

INGREDIENTS

2¼ CUPS BREAD FLOUR

1 TEASPOON BAKING SODA

1 TEASPOON SALT

1 CUP SALTED BUTTER, BROWNED

½ CUP MAPLE SUGAR

¾ CUP BROWN SUGAR

½ TEASPOON VANILLA EXTRACT

3.4-OUNCE BOX OF VANILLA PUDDING MIX

2 EGGS + 1 EGG YOLK

2 CUPS SEMI-SWEET CHOCOLATE CHIPS

<u>INSTRUCTIONS</u>

1. Line a cookie sheet with parchment paper or a silicone baking mat.
2. combine flour, baking soda, and salt in a small bowl with a spoon.
3. Brown butter in a small pot over low heat, continuing to stir and supervise until butter melts and turns from yellow to light brown. It burns quickly, so I recommend not walking away until it's removed from the heat.
4. In a mixer, beat together the browned butter, maple sugar, brown sugar, vanilla extract, vanilla pudding powder, and eggs until well-blended.
5. Stir in the flour mixture.
6. Add the chocolate chips and mix just until spread evenly throughout the dough.
7. Use a small ice cream scooper to evenly space cookies on the baking sheet. Leave at least two inches between drops of dough because the cookies will be larger than normal.
8. Bake at 350°F for 7–9 minutes or until cookie edges begin to brown. Centers will be soft and cloud-like.
9. Cool cookies on a wire rack.
10. Serve with a very cold glass of milk or a cup of hot tea.

LEMON BARS

Book 3: Three Times to Make Sure
Chapter 9

The ladies from Janie Lyn and Maree's Mah Jongg group had asked to be in charge of the desserts. M'Kenzee had gladly agreed; then they blew her away with what they'd accomplished. A stunning three-tiered wedding cake with edible pearls and fresh roses acted as the centerpiece on an oversized wooden worktable they'd found in the barn's storeroom. They'd draped it in gauzy white fabric and added white, cream, silver, and gold candles in varying shapes and heights. The candlelight cast a soft glow over large white platters of homemade cookies, brownies, and lemon bars, which surrounded the gorgeous cake. The smell of sugar and heaven wafted throughout the barn.

———

I'll confess, aside from a refreshing glass of lemonade, I'm not a big fan of lemon. But I know I'm in the minority, and I love cooking and baking for others, so I've made this lemon bar recipe on multiple occasions, and it always receives rave reviews.

I included this recipe in Janie Lyn and Maxwell's wedding reception because when the community came together to produce their surprise party, I know the tables were gorgeous and colorful! They would have looked bright and beautiful with the pop of yellow these lemon bars provide.

I do love a pretty table!

On top of that, this recipe is so easy, you'll read it twice worrying you missed a step somewhere. Nope… You've done it just right. These lemon bars are just that simple.

CRUST INGREDIENTS

2 CUPS PASTRY FLOUR

1 CUP SALTED BUTTER, CUBED AND KEPT COLD

½ CUP GRANULATED SUGAR

⅓ CUP POWDERED SUGAR

FILLING INGREDIENTS

2 CUPS GRANULATED SUGAR

⅓ CUP ALL-PURPOSE FLOUR

4 EGGS + 1 YOLK

3 LEMONS, ZESTED AND JUICED

TOPPING INGREDIENT

POWDERED SUGAR

INSTRUCTIONS

1. LINE A 9" x 13" BAKING DISH WITH PARCHMENT PAPER AND SET ASIDE.

2. USING A FOOD PROCESSOR, PULSE TOGETHER PASTRY FLOUR, GRANULATED SUGAR, AND POWDERED SUGAR.

3. ADD CUBED BUTTER AND PULSE A FEW MORE TIMES OR UNTIL THE MIXTURE IS CRUMBLY WITH SMALL BITS OF BUTTER VISIBLE.

4. PRESS CRUST MIXTURE INTO THE BAKING DISH, MAKING SURE TO PUSH DOUGH FULLY INTO THE CORNERS (SO THE LEMON CURD DOESN'T SEEP UNDERNEATH THE CRUST).

5. BAKE CRUST AT 350°F FOR 15-20 MINUTES OR UNTIL EDGES ARE JUST TURNING GOLDEN BROWN.

6. WHILE CRUST IS BAKING, MIX LEMON CURD FILLING.

7. COMBINE GRANULATED SUGAR, ALL-PURPOSE FLOUR, EGGS, 2 TABLESPOONS LEMON ZEST, AND ALL THE LEMON JUICE EXTRACTED FROM THE FRUIT IN A MIXER. PROCESS UNTIL WELL-BLENDED.

8. WHEN CRUST IS FINISHED BAKING, IMMEDIATELY POUR LEMON CURD INTO THE CRUST AND RETURN TO OVEN.

9. BAKE AT 350°F FOR AN ADDITIONAL 17-22 MINUTES OR UNTIL LEMON CURD IS SET BUT STILL SOFT (IT WILL CONTINUE TO SET WHILE COOLING).

10. REMOVE FROM OVEN WHEN FINISHED BAKING.

11. COOL IN ROOM TEMPERATURE FOR ONE HOUR AND COOL IN REFRIGERATOR FOR 2–3 HOURS.

12. ONCE CHILLED, SLICE INTO 20 SMALL BARS. PLACE BARS ON PLATTER OR TRAY.

13. DUST WITH POWDERED SUGAR RIGHT BEFORE SERVING.

MAREE'S STRAWBERRY JAM

Book 1: Grocery Girl
Chapter 8

"This jelly!" Davis commented slathering another healthy heap on top of his bagel.

"It's strawberry jam. Maree made it."

"Maree made it?"

Rhys couldn't keep himself from smiling. Again. This seemed to be happening quite a bit. He didn't think he minded that fact as much now, at least not as much as he had at first. Maybe.

This strawberry jam recipe is really where it all began...

My daughter, Maci Maree, learned to make jam in third grade. By sixth grade, she'd perfected this recipe. She even used it for her science fair project that year. To say it's scrumptious is a tragic understatement.

There is no telling how many jars of strawberry jam we've made together — somewhere in the hundreds, no doubt. Possible thousands! That alone makes this the most special recipe in the book, at least to me.

Maci inspired so much of Book 1, *The Davenports* miniseries, and my entire writing adventure; it's only fitting she's also featured in our first Green Hills cookbook.

Have fun with this jam recipe, and be sure you make plenty. Your family will thank you.

PS: I love you, Angel Girl!

INGREDIENTS

2–3 QUARTS STRAWBERRIES

6 CUPS GRANULATED SUGAR

3 TABLESPOONS LEMON JUICE

1.75-OUNCE BOX OF POWDERED PECTIN

½ TEASPOON BUTTER OR MARGARINE

(REDUCES FOAMING)

INSTRUCTIONS

1. REMOVE STRAWBERRY STEMS AND LEAVES. RINSE FRUIT WELL.
2. USING A CHINOIS OR SIEVE, MASH AND STRAIN THE STRAWBERRIES TO EXTRACT 6 CUPS OF JUICE.
3. COMBINE STRAWBERRY JUICE, LEMON JUICE, AND SUGAR IN AN 8-QUART DUTCH OVEN OR LARGE STOCK POT. STIR WELL AND BRING TO A ROLLING BOIL THAT WON'T STIR DOWN.
4. COOK 1 MINUTE, STIRRING CONTINUOUSLY.
5. ADD PECTIN AND BUTTER; RETURN TO A HARD ROLLING BOIL OVER HIGH HEAT (AGAIN, CANNOT BE STIRRED DOWN); STIR FREQUENTLY.
6. CONTINUE BOILING FOR 1–2 MINUTES. USING A METAL SPOON, TEST FOR DONENESS. JAM IS READY WHEN A FEW DROPS OF MIXTURE REMAIN ON THE SIDE OF THE SPOON OR SLIDES OFF THE SPOON IN A SHEET.
7. REMOVE FROM HEAT; SKIM OFF ANY FOAM WITH METAL SPOON.
8. QUICKLY LADLE JAM INTO HOT, STERILIZED JARS, LEAVING ¼-INCH HEADSPACE.
9. COVER WITH CANNING LID AND RING; SCREW BANDS TIGHTLY.
10. PROCESS IN BOILING WATER BATH FOR 10 MINUTES.
11. REMOVE JARS FROM CANNER; LET COOL FOR 24 HOURS.
12. CHECK LIDS AND TIGHTEN RINGS AGAIN AS NEEDED.
13. JAM CAN BE STORED IN A COOL, DRY PLACE FOR UP TO 12 MONTHS.

PEANUT BUTTER COOKIES

Book 4: Take a Chance on Love
Chapter 2

"Is that basket from Miss Sadie?" Davis asked.

"What basket?" Landry asked, faking a confused expression.

"The one sitting next to your chair," he pointed out.

"Oh, my basket? Yes, Miss Sadie filled it — for me — before I left this morning. Hot soup, homemade cookies— You should've smelled them coming out of the oven." Landry closed her eyes, inhaling the crisp air and remembering the scent of fresh baked cookies with rapture.

"I smell them now," Davis supplied. "Peanut butter, I'm guessing."

"Mmmm— Yes."

"And are you planning on sharing your basket?" Davis oozed charm as he smiled at Landry.

"I imagine that depends. What will you give me?" She enjoyed tossing the saucy challenge his way.

———

I knew Landry and Davis would end up together from the moment they met at Scooters in Book 1. But, alas, they had to wait their turn! This scene from the beginning of their love story was a blast to write because it highlights how their "fun and flirty friendship" had no choice but to develop into a life together and a love to last forever.

INGREDIENTS

½ CUP GRANULATED SUGAR

1 ¼ CUPS ALL-PURPOSE FLOUR

¾ TEASPOON BAKING SODA

½ TEASPOON BAKING POWDER

¼ TEASPOON SALT

¾ CUP BROWN SUGAR

¾ CUP PEANUT SALTED BUTTER

¼ CUP SHORTENING

¼ CUP BUTTER, SOFTENED

1 EGG

1 TEASPOON VANILLA EXTRACT

<u>INSTRUCTIONS</u>

1. COMBINE GRANULATED SUGAR, FLOUR, BAKING SODA, BAKING POWDER, AND SALT IN A SMALL BOWL. SIFT OR STIR TOGETHER. SET ASIDE.

2. MIX BROWN SUGAR, BUTTER, SHORTENING, EGG, AND VANILLA IN A LARGE BOWL.

3. STIR IN DRY INGREDIENT MIX UNTIL MOIST. DO NOT OVER-MIX OR COOKIES WILL BE TOUGH.

4. COVER BOWL AND REFRIGERATE DOUGH FOR 20–30 MINUTES TO LIGHTLY CHILL.

5. ROLL DOUGH INTO SMALL BALLS (1½" OR JUST A TINY BIT SMALLER THAN A PING PONG BALL).

6. PLACE THE DOUGH BALLS 2 INCHES APART ON AN UNGREASED COOKIE SHEET.

7. USING A FORK, CREATE THE TRADITIONAL CROSS-HATCHING DESIGN ON TOP OF EACH COOKIE BY LIGHTLY PRESSING DOWN THE DOUGH. THIS TECHNIQUE ENSURES A NICE, EVEN BAKE. YOU CAN DIP THE FORK IN GRANULATED SUGAR BEFORE FLATTENING TO ADD GLAMOUR TO YOUR COOKIE TOPS.

8. BAKE AT 375°F FOR 7–8 MINUTES OR UNTIL LIGHTLY GOLDEN ON THE EDGES.

9. COOL ON BAKING SHEET 2–3 MINUTES BEFORE TRANSFERRING COOKIES TO A COOLING RACK. LET BAKING SHEET COOL COMPLETELY BETWEEN BATCHES SO DOUGH DOESN'T MELT WHEN PLACED ON A WARM PAN. I SET THE DOUGH BACK IN THE FRIDGE TO CHILL BETWEEN BAKES.

QUICK BAKED BREAD

Book 2: In the Trenches
Chapter 7

"How can I help?"

Maxwell stood hip-to-hip with her at the sink, reaching across her to squirt soap into his hands, and then working the soap into a lather that he rubbed through his fingers, around both wrists, and a good six inches up his fore-arms. It was riveting. She couldn't drag her eyes away.

"Well?" He reached across her again to snatch the tea towel she'd set on the counter. Her eyes followed the motion until he dried his hands, bent at the elbows, so that her eyes also caught the fine form of his chest under the plain white shirt he still wore with his swim trunks.

When she finally forced her eyes up to his face, his smile deepened to yet another degree. She froze in place, utterly speechless.

Until he winked. Knowing she was making a fool of herself, and knowing he knew it as well snapped Janie Lyn's attention from the hypnotic effect he had over her. She snatched the towel from his hands — which only made him chuckle — and turned back to her vegetables, the cutting board, and a sharp chef's knife.

"I'll chop these if you want to pull the ingredients to start the bread."

Surely, I can think rationally enough to remember the recipe, she thought to herself.

But of course she could. She'd made this a thousand times, maybe a million. She could bake this bread in her sleep…which was a little how she felt. The entire afternoon had been a dream, one she hoped never to awaken from, so it never had to end.

"Let me guess — flour, sugar, and eggs?"

In romance novels, mindless and mundane tasks take on a whole new meaning. This scene is a great example of how that works — as well as Landry's introduction to quilt block trimming in Book 4!

Maxwell's presence shrank the normally spacious kitchen, sent Janie Lyn's nerves buzzing, and turned her mind to mush. Luckily, this incredible bread recipe proved to be frazzle-proof.

I enjoyed writing it in equal proportion to how much I enjoy baking — and indulging in — this bread recipe. It's wonderful sliced thin for a sandwich, sliced thick for French toast, or simply buttered with a dollop of Maree's Strawberry Jam.

One word of advice: when you take the time to bake it, you might as well make two batches because one loaf rarely survives the first ten minutes it's out of the oven.

<u>INGREDIENTS</u>

2½ CUPS BREAD FLOUR + EXTRA AS NEEDED
1 HEAPING TABLESPOON GRANULATED SUGAR
1 TEASPOON SALT
1, 1-OUNCE PACKET DRY YEAST
¾ CUP WATER
3 TABLESPOONS OIL + A DRIZZLE FOR THE RISE
3 EGGS, ROOM TEMPERATURE
2–3 SPRIGS FRESH ROSEMARY
COURSE SEA SALT

<u>INSTRUCTIONS</u>

1. STIR TOGETHER 2½ CUPS FLOUR, SUGAR, REGULAR SALT, AND YEAST IN A LARGE BOWL (OR USE A STAND MIXER AND DOUGH HOOK).
2. IN A SMALL SAUCEPAN, HEAT WATER AND OIL OVER MEDIUM HEAT UNTIL THE WATER STARTS TO RADIATE HEAT. IT DOES NOT NEED TO BOIL; ONCE A HAND HELD 10–12 INCHES OVER THE PAN FEELS HEAT FROM THE WATER, IT'S READY.
3. WHILE WAITING FOR THE LIQUID MIXTURE TO WARM, ADD 2 EGGS TO THE DRY MIXTURE AND MIX GENTLY (OR ON MEDIUM SETTING).
4. POUR THE WARM LIQUID MIXTURE INTO THE DRY MIXTURE.
5. BLEND MIXTURE BY HAND (OR WITH A BREAD HOOK ON MEDIUM SETTING) UNTIL IT FORMS A SOFT DOUGH.

6. Turn dough onto a lightly floured work surface. Knead the dough until it forms a ball the texture of smooth elastic (usually takes 6–8 minutes or about 300 kneads).

7. Drizzle a small bit of oil in a mixing bowl. Add the dough ball to the bowl, coating it in the oil. Cover with a clean tea towel and set aside in a warm spot or a proofing drawer.

8. The dough should rise to double its size in about 90 minutes.

9. Once risen to that size, it's time to punch down the air bubbles.

10. Using 2 sprigs of rosemary, break off the needles by sliding your fingers down the stem. Add the needles to the dough.

11. Make a fist and press it into the center of the dough. Pull the edges of the dough back to the center to shape the dough into another ball. Continue punching down the air bubbles and dispersing the rosemary needles. Just a few more times is enough.

12. Turn the dough onto a lightly floured work surface. Divide it into thirds.

13. Using ⅓, create 3 dough strips. Braid the three together and set the rope aside.

14. Using the remaining ⅔ of the original dough ball, braid a thicker rope.

15. Stack the small rope on top of the thicker one, tuck under the ends, and set aside to rise for 30–40 minutes or until doubled in size again.

16. When ready, mix the leftover egg with 2 tablespoons of water to create an egg wash. Brush or paint the egg wash over the braided

AND STACKED LOAF. IF YOU HAVE ANY ROSEMARY LEFT, SPRINKLE A LITTLE OVER THE TOP OF THE BRAID.

17. BAKE BREAD LOAF AT 375°F FOR 25–30 MINUTES OR UNTIL CRUST IS GOLDEN BROWN. IF IT BROWNS TOO QUICKLY, TENT TIN FOIL OVER THE TOP TO MAINTAIN ITS WARM, BUTTERY COLOR.

18. REMOVE FROM OVEN AND PLACE LOAF ON A RACK TO COOL.

19. SLICE OR TEAR TO SERVE.

SOPAPILLA CHEESECAKE

Book 1: Grocery Girl
Chapter 22

inner was fantastic. Not counting the few meals that Maree had cooked for Rhys and Max, it was the first "normal" family-style dinner that Rhys had experienced since before the fire. Sadie had made an incredible tray of sour cream beef enchiladas with homemade tamales on the side, chips and queso, a fabulous taco salad, and sopapilla cheesecake for dessert...

———

On the heels of a harsh realization, Rhys needed time to heal. A wonderful dinner with special people and a sweet dessert delivered the perfect therapy.

Indeed, this dressed-up cheesecake never disappoints, and it always lifts chins and bolsters courage.

A dear family friend made this for us decades ago, and I simply had to have the recipe. Since then, I've made Sopapilla Cheesecake no fewer than a hundred times. And while I've seen other versions of the recipe, this is still my favorite way to make it.

It travels well, goes with any cuisine, and is very simple to create. Best of all, it is lovely and tastes divine!

INGREDIENTS

2 CANS OF CRESCENT ROLLS
3, 8-OUNCE PACKAGES OF CREAM CHEESE
1 1/2 CUPS SUGAR
1 TEASPOON VANILLA EXTRACT
1/2 STICK BUTTER, MELTED
SUGAR & CINNAMON TO SPRINKLE ON TOP

INSTRUCTIONS

1. UNROLL ONE CAN OF CRESCENT ROLLS INTO THE BOTTOM OF A 9" X 13" BAKING DISH.
2. PRESS SEAMS TOGETHER.
3. CREAM TOGETHER THE CREAM CHEESE, 1 1/2 CUPS SUGAR, AND VANILLA EXTRACT.
4. SPREAD MIXTURE ON TOP OF ROLLS.
5. UNROLL SECOND CAN OF ROLLS ON TOP OF MIXTURE AND PINCH SEAMS TOGETHER.
6. TOP WITH MELTED BUTTER AND SPRINKLE WITH A GOOD COATING OF CINNAMON AND SUGAR.
7. BAKE AT 325°F FOR 30-35 MINUTES OR UNTIL GOLDEN BROWN.

BEVERAGES

I grew up in the south. As an adult, I've always lived in the south. And in the south, gravy does indeed go with every meal.

But it's not a beverage.

And while our friends in Green Hills love comfort food — like gravy — they have a few *other* favorite beverages to share...

AUNT KAY'S PEACH TEA

Book 1: Grocery Girl
Chapter 20

"What to drink?" he asked, walking back toward the kitchen.

"A cup of hot tea?" she ventured, not sure if he drank tea. Or coffee, for that matter. She loved him, and believed they shared a meaningful connection, but she still had quite a lot to learn about Rhys Larsen.

"I can do that," he called from the other room, and returned a few minutes later with a massive glass of cold milk for himself and an oversized mug of heated sweet tea for her. Not a fancy tea set or flavored bags that needed to steep, but a glass of sweet iced tea that had been poured into a mug and heated in the microwave. It was perfect, and she readily admitted — only in her mind, of course — that she was smitten.

———

This peach tea is really more like a fizzy fruity punch one might serve at a shower or party, and it's addictive!

My sister-in-law, Kay, introduced the recipe to our family years ago, and now I keep the ingredients in the pantry *at all times*.

I often make it to enjoy myself, I always m a pitcher for football dinners, and my daughter has taken it to school for numerous class events. No matter what time of year, who's in attendance, or what cuisine is being served, it's always a big hit.

Try it over a glass of ice or heating it like Rhys does for Maree in Book 1. Either way, you'll love it.

INGREDIENTS

2 LITERS GINGER ALE
1 PITCHER PACK CRYSTAL LIGHT® PEACH ICED TEA
DRINK MIX
SMALL JAR OF WATER

INSTRUCTIONS

1. IN THE SMALL JAR, DISSOLVE POWDERED DRINK MIX IN ABOUT 2 OUNCES OF WATER.
2. SLOWLY POUR THE TEA MIXTURE AND THE GINGER ALE INTO A PITCHER.
3. STIR GENTLY.
4. SERVE OVER ICE.

CHRISTMAS WASSAIL

Book 3: Three Times to Make Sure
Chapter 17

"So, you — Max's brilliant, gorgeous, and fierce new wife — are going into business with Mary Beth Carmichael — Max's brilliant, gorgeous, and fierce ex-girlfriend? That's quite a strategy… Keep your friends close and your enemies closer, huh?"

"Oh, no. It's nothing like that," Janie Lyn laughed, waving off the notion that Mary Beth could ever be an enemy. "Maxwell never felt that way about Mary Beth — they really didn't date for more than a week or so. She's been such a wonderful friend to us both. I just adore her!"

"So, Lyndale Christmas Cakes will be back with a vengeance next year? What else will The Christmas Collection consist of?"

M'Kenzee enjoyed listening to Janie Lyn go on about their plans. Janie Lyn had a knack for storytelling; M'Kenzee easily envisioned the kitchen with its bakery counter and soda-shop-style interior, the restaurant with its inviting atmosphere and savory comfort foods, and the gift shop stuffed full of Christmas decor, artificial trees and baskets of ornaments, barrels of ribbons and holiday picks, and the upstairs section of quilts and holiday fabrics that Maree had agreed to help curate and maintain. It would be fabulous, and it would bring a healthy caravan of shoppers to Green Hills just in time to help the local economy surge through the winter.

"Have you thought of planting a tree farm?" M'Kenzee blinked rapidly; her question surprised them both.

"Well, no. But it's a fantastic idea," Janie Lyn pondered. "Perhaps with a clearing for picnic tables where we could serve wassail and hot chocolate?"

———

All the wonderful ideas Janie Lyn and M'Kenzee share in the scene above provide a sneak peek into a new Green Hills holiday tradition: The Christmas Collection.

Beginning with *Book 5: Undeveloped Love* in 2023, I plan to release Green Hills holiday love stories in the form of seasonal novellas for a very long time. The shortened format is perfect for curling up in front of a fireplace — perhaps under a Green Hills quilt — for a few hours between the myriad of activities that keep us hustling and bustling from Halloween to Valentine's Day.

We all need to press the pause button from time to time, and what better way to catch our breath than a sweet romance?

Trust me when I say… You've earned a break, and this wassail recipe is the perfect companion to an afternoon of reading and relaxing!

<u>INGREDIENTS</u>

8 CUPS APPLE CIDER

4½ CUPS PINEAPPLE JUICE

2½ CUPS ORANGE JUICE

½ CUP CRANBERRY JUICE

½ CUP LEMON JUICE

3 TABLESPOONS HONEY

3 CINNAMON STICKS

2 TEASPOONS CLOVES

¼ TEASPOON GROUND GINGER

¼ TEASPOON GROUND NUTMEG

SLICED FRUIT FOR GARNISH

(APPLES, ORANGES, PEACHES & PLUMS WORK WELL)

<u>INSTRUCTIONS</u>

1. COMBINE ALL INGREDIENTS (EXCEPT THE FRUIT FOR GARNISH) IN A STOCK POT OR DUTCH OVEN.
2. SIMMER OVER LOW TO MEDIUM HEAT FOR 20-25 MINUTES.
3. STRAIN AND LADLE INTO MUGS.
4. ADD A SLICE OR TWO OF FRUIT TO EACH MUG BEFORE SERVING.

PERFECTLY SWEET TEA

Book 2: In the Trenches
Chapter 1

He grabbed his bag from the back seat, unlocked the side door of the house, and opened the fridge, looking for something to drink. His day improved another notch when he saw that someone had been at the house and left an almost-full pitcher of sweet tea. He grabbed an insulated cup, filled it with ice, and poured tea to the rim. He took a long, deep drink, then refilled the tumbler and set the lid in place.

He planned to hop through the shower, grab swim trunks, and hit his new pool. He'd helped design it last winter, but he'd not yet seen the project finished. Janie Lyn had a landscape architect finishing the green spaces, but the pool was ready. Max could not wait to jump in.

Refreshed from his shower, he put on the shorts, grabbed his tea and his sunglasses, and walked toward the wall of glass windows and doors over-looking the backyard from the living room.

Max was shocked to find someone already out there. Not just someone, but some woman!

———

There is very little my sweet husband asks for in this life! In fact, his list goes something like this…

1. BE HAPPY TO SEE ME WHEN I GET HOME.
2. MAKE SURE I GET UP WHEN MY ALARM GOES OFF IN THE MORNING.
3. ALWAYS HAVE SWEET TEA IN THE FRIDGE.

At our house — and in Green Hills — sweet tea is a way of life. Here's our recipe for the perfect pitcher.

INGREDIENTS

4 CUPS WATER
2 FAMILY SIZE LIPTON® TEA BAGS
1 CUP SUGAR

INSTRUCTIONS

1. COMBINE WATER AND TEA BAGS IN A LARGE GLASS MEASURING CUP.
2. MICROWAVE ON HIGH FOR $3\frac{1}{2}$ MINUTES.
3. LET SIT FOR 6–7 MINUTES TO BREW.
4. WHILE IT BREWS, POUR THE SUGAR INTO A GALLON-SIZED PITCHER AND FILL IT ABOUT $\frac{3}{4}$ WITH WARM WATER.

5. Stir vigorously until sugar is completely dissolved.
6. Add the tea mixture and stir to mix.
7. Top-off pitcher with cold water.
8. Store in refrigerator.
9. Serve over ice.

TRIPLE T'S MILKSHAKE

Book 4: Take a Chance on Love
Chapter 10

"What's going on, buddy?" Davis set the gift bag he'd been carrying on the floor and walked to Zane's bed.

"Today's my birthday," Zane replied, in the most depressing rendition of today's my birthday that Davis had ever heard.

"I know," Davis said, reaching for the birthday present to set it on Zane's bed. "Isn't that a good thing?"

"I thought maybe my dad would call," Zane whispered. "And I have to leave."

"Your dad's going through a lot of tough treatments, working hard to get home to be with you. I'm sure he'll call tonight if there's any way possible. And if you don't hear from him today, I know he'll be eager to celebrate your birthday as soon as he's back from Dallas. Eddie's always up for a *fun birthday dinner," Davis said, ruffling the boy's hair in camaraderie. "Now, what's this about leaving?"*

At that, Landry turned from the window and faced the boys.

"Zane's doing so well that he's ready to go home." Landry's voice fell short of sounding upbeat.

"But I don't have anywhere to go," Zane added. His chin dropped to his chest, and his voice quivered.

Davis's gaze darted to Landry.

"We're working on that, Zane," she promised. "You're going to be just fine, sweetie. Don't you worry about a thing." Her voice quivered, too. And Davis caught her swiping her cheek before she walked to the opposite side of Zane's bed. "I've got rounds on the fourth floor, and then I'll be back with your special order: cheeseburger, curly fries, plenty of ketchup, and a strawberry milkshake," she said with a fake smile plastered on her face. "Davis, will you be joining us for dinner tonight?"

"There's nowhere else I'd rather be," he exclaimed. "How about I set this present over there — out of reach of curious birthday boys — and pick up the to-go order? I can be back before Doctor Stark finishes with her rounds, and we'll all meet here to sing, blow out candles, and make birthday wishes."

Zane brightened, and a genuine grin blossomed across his face.

———

We've been hearing about the milkshakes from The Three-Toed Turtle since Book 1, and they sound pretty amazing every time they pop up on a page.

In the scene above, Earl's strawberry milkshake is just what the doctor ordered to cheer up a birthday boy with a big heart and a heavy burden.

*P*ersonally, plain ol' vanilla is my favorite flavor, so that's the recipe I'm sharing below. But never fear, I've included a whole list of add-ins to dress up your Triple T's Milkshake for each of your loved ones.

<u>INGREDIENTS</u>

¼ CUP DRIED PITTED DATES, CHOPPED

1 CUP COLD MILK

2 CUPS VANILLA ICE CREAM

¼ TEASPOON GRATED NUTMEG

<u>INSTRUCTIONS</u>

1. COMBINE ALL INGREDIENTS IN BLENDER.
2. PROCESS UNTIL SHAKE IS SMOOTH.

<u>OPTIONAL ADD-INS</u>

1 CUP STRAWBERRIES

3 OREO® COOKIES

2 TABLESPOONS CHOCOLATE SYRUP

3 TABLESPOONS CREAMY PEANUT BUTTER

3 TABLESPOONS NUTELLA®

1 FROZEN BANANA

2 FUN SIZE BUTTERFINGER® CANDY BARS

MUSIC PLAYLIST

All music is beautiful.
Billy Strayhorn

*E*njoy these food-based tunes while cooking and baking with the Green Hills characters…

1. Food is the Dream - Dan Evans-Parker
2. Sing for Your Supper - The Mamas & The Papas
3. Strawberry Wine - Deana Carter
4. Spaghetti - salem ilese
5. dinner alone - Arny Margret
6. Make it with You - Bread
7. Bread - Lukrembo
8. Buttered Popcorn - The Supremes
9. Copper Kettle - Rick, Robin & Him
10. Home Cookin' - Jr. Walker & The All Stars
11. Mashed Potato Popcorn - James Brown
12. Red Red Wine - UB40
13. Jambalaya (On the Bayou) - Carpenters
14. Vegetables - The Beach Boys

15. Cheeseburger in Paradise - Jimmy Buffett
16. Banana Boat (Day-O) - Harry Belafonte
17. Tacos, Enchiladas and Beans - Doris Day, George Sirava and His Orchestra
18. Country Pie - Bob Dylan
19. Savoy Truffle - Ella Fitzgerald
20. Sugar - Flo Rida and Wynter Gordon
21. Suga Suga - Baby Bash and Frankie J
22. Banana Pancakes - Jack Johnson
23. Lollipop - The Chordates
24. Banana Split for My Baby - Louis Prima, Keely Smith, Sam Butera & The Witnesses
25. The Muffin Man - Ella Fitzgerald & Her Famous Orchestra
26. Marshmallow - Lukrembo

Available on Spotify as
"The Davenports EAT by Virginia'dele Smith"

ABOUT THE AUTHOR

Ashli Montgomery is a wife, a momma, and an author whose passion is sharing love stories, books, quilts, yoga, recipes, and all of her favorite things in life. She is quilting to mend the mind by spearheading a community of quilters through Quilt 2 End ALZ, Inc., a 501(c)(3) nonprofit she launched to use her quilting hobby as a platform to advocate for an end to Alzheimer's disease.

Ashli writes wholesome and cozy romance under the pen name Virginia'dele Smith to honor Syble Virginia Tidwell, Adele Gertrude Baylin, and Etta Jean Smith. These three cherished grandmothers were beautiful role models, teaching Ashli to love without judgment and to always put family first. Through Grandma Syble's journals and appetite for books, through Momadele's priceless cards and handwritten letters, and through many, many hours of visiting over fabric at Mema's kitchen island, Ashli also learned to treasure words.

Get to know Ashli by subscribing to her newsletter, *The Gazette*, at AshliMontgomery.com